PROJECT TERRA
CRASH COURSE

PENGUIN WORKSHOP
Penguin Young Readers Group
An Imprint of Penguin Random House LLC

Penguin supports copyright. Copyright fuels creativity, encourages
diverse voices, promotes free speech, and creates a vibrant culture.
Thank you for buying an authorized edition of this book and for
complying with copyright laws by not reproducing, scanning,
or distributing any part of it in any form without permission.
You are supporting writers and allowing Penguin to continue to publish
books for every reader.

The publisher does not have any control over and does not assume any
responsibility for author or third-party websites or their content.

Copyright © 2017 Penguin Random House LLC. All rights reserved.
Published by Penguin Workshop, an imprint of Penguin Random House LLC,
345 Hudson Street, New York, New York 10014. PENGUIN and
PENGUIN WORKSHOP are trademarks of Penguin Books Ltd,
and the W colophon is a trademark of Penguin Random House LLC.
Printed in the USA.

Book design by Kayla Wasil.

Library of Congress Cataloging-in-Publication Data is available.

ISBN 9780515157918   10 9 8 7 6 5 4 3 2 1

PROJECT TERRA

CRASH COURSE

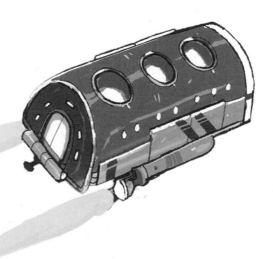

BY LANDRY Q. WALKER

illustrated by Keith Zoo

Penguin Workshop
An Imprint of Penguin Random House

Many thanks go to my editor, Max Bisantz, for his patience and guidance, and Liz Marsham and John Adams for their help. And also thanks to Eric Jones—because credit where credit is due—LQW

For Zoey, my little space explorer—KZ

CHAPTER 001

Elara Adele Vaughn sat in the empty shuttle station.

The large gray-and-white terminal was deserted, but the young girl wasn't alone. She stared into the holographic projection of her little brother, Danny.

"It's not like it's super far," Elara said, "and you get to come visit during break. That's just a few months away."

The shimmering blue, transparent image of Danny

didn't look convinced. He was three years younger than Elara—having just turned nine—and small for his age. Danny was obviously upset, but he shrugged and half smiled anyway. "I guess," he said. "Maybe you'll change your mind. Maybe you'll transfer."

Elara felt herself frown. She didn't want to fight. Not right now. Not with her little brother. But she knew where Danny was hearing this from—her parents.

"You're so good at farming," Danny pushed. "And mom and dad say the Affiliation needs farmers. They say you could get a grant—"

"The Affiliation needs terraformers, too," Elara said, gently cutting her brother off. "More than anything. If we don't expand our borders and colonize more worlds, where will we farm?"

For as long as Elara could remember, she wanted to become a terraformer. Specifically, she wanted to be a bioengineer and learn to create new life-forms on new worlds. That wasn't something Elara could achieve on her home world—Vega Antilles V, a remote farming community on the fringes of Sector 17. A planet so far away it was usually called "Nowhere." It also wasn't something she could do by attending the Academy of Agriculture, which was where all her older brothers and sisters went. It was probably where Danny would go too, when he was older.

"I guess you have to go then," Danny said sadly. "You can't blame me for not liking it, though."

Elara felt her smile return. It was true. How mad could she get at her little brother for missing her? "Well, I'll come and visit. I promise you that. And the Seven Systems School of Terraforming has a break the same week you do, and you'll come visit me then. Right?"

"The name of the school is 'STS,'" Danny said. "No one says it like that except you."

"It's a very important school!" Elara said in mock offense. "The Seven Systems School is the leading educator of terraformers!"

Danny rolled his eyes. "You sound like one of their ads. 'The Seven Systems School of Terraforming Sciences and Arts: Create your own world!'"

Elara stuck her tongue out in response.

Danny waved his hands dramatically, the hologram sparkling more as it animated the motion. "Your journey begins . . . NOW!"

"Well, it is a good slogan," Elara responded, standing up from her bench and grabbing her heavy backpack. "And it happens to be true. Literally. My train just got here."

"Oh. Okay . . . ," Danny said. It was clear he wasn't ready to end the conversation. Neither was Elara. But interplanetary communications were limited and costly. Projecting them during hypertravel was virtually impossible. Time was ticking . . .

Suddenly Elara felt overwhelmed. Her heart raced, and she felt her brow furrow. Leaving was more difficult than she had expected. Her family had dropped her off hours ago and said their goodbyes. Her brothers. Her sisters. Her mom and her dad. Maybe they didn't entirely understand why Elara was leaving, but they still supported her decision. They all stood at the platform and hugged her one by one. They were a large family. A poor family by most standards. But they were loving and hardworking and happy. And they were hers. And now . . .

"Hey," Danny said, sensing his sister's mood shift. "Hey. It's okay. You're right . . . it's just a few months until you have Visitors Day. I'll be there to see you. Mom and Dad already booked the trip for me."

Elara smiled, her hand reaching out to touch the blue light of Danny's holographic projection.

"I'll miss you," Elara said, her eyes rimmed with tears. "Lots. Every day. And I will write you all the time. I promise."

"Double promise?" Danny asked.

"Always. Forever and ever."

Danny smiled again, and the connection was cut off. And for the first time in her entire young life, Elara really was alone.

CHAPTER 002

The doors of the shuttle train hissed open, belching tiny clouds of bluish gas down the length of the transport. Elara stood for a moment, steeling herself as the vehicle hummed. Taking a deep breath, the future student of the Seven Systems School of Terraforming Sciences and Arts stepped aboard the small shuttle, and the doors closed behind her.

Inside, the shuttle was empty and quiet. Elara made her way to an open seat. She buckled in and steadied herself for what turned out to be a surprisingly smooth takeoff.

The space vehicle was controlled by computer, and so for the first hour of her long journey, Elara was completely alone. Rows of empty seats stretched out around her. This wasn't too surprising. Not many people came and went from Sector 17. Not enough habitable planets existed that far out from the Core of the Affiliated Worlds.

Elara tapped absently at the communications control pad at her seat. Inactive. No long-range or short-range communications would be possible.

It was weird: Life on the farm could be so quiet. Vega Antilles V was a large planet with a tiny population. But quiet on a living world versus quiet in the middle of space . . . that was different.

It was peaceful.

Elara looked at her own faint reflection in the plexiglass window, shaking her mop of thick purple hair as she did. Her image was surrounded by the gently swirling colors of deep hyperspace, which she found soothing.

And then it was abruptly over.

Elara felt the gravitational pull of a planet, her stomach lurching like she was on a carnival ride. The shuttle was descending onto another world. An entire ecosystem, completely new and unfamiliar. Elara felt her fingers tighten around the end of her seat's armrest in excitement. She had never been off Vega Antilles V before. Sure, she had seen travel holograms and experienced other biospheres that way. But Elara knew it wouldn't be the same as actually being on another planet.

Elara rose from her seat and made her way to the shuttle doors. Punching up the manifest on the data pad, she took note of the planet name—Thui Prime, only recently discovered and designated a mining world by the Affiliation. It was an exportation hub for fuel and gases. *That made sense*, Elara thought. They were still too deep in the outer rim for the wealthier worlds. Industrial and agricultural planets were most common this far out.

"A brand-new planet . . . ," Elara whispered to herself as she stared out the window. Everything she had left behind . . . Nothing would take that sting away. Not completely. But this was the reward. No one in her family had ever set foot on another planet. Not in four generations, since back when her great-great-grandparents Pannel and Samantha Vaughn had accepted placement on Vega Antilles V in the space-colonization program. No one had seen a point in leaving.

As the shuttle landed on Thui Prime's station platform, Elara could see the bright green of the tall, thin trees just outside the station—very different from anything they had on Vega Antilles V. The sky was different, too, just on the brighter side of purple. It was a lush and colorful world, and Elara couldn't wait to experience it firsthand. Thumbing the unlock button, she stepped forward to take in her first breath of otherworldly air . . .

. . . and choked back the most awful stench she had ever smelled!

Frantically, Elara tapped at the shuttle's data pad, and the doors slid shut. Gagging, she rubbed her stinging eyes. Right. Gas planet. A planet where they harvest gas. From boggy, festering pools of methane-rich liquid. Technically, the air was breathable, or the shuttle would never have landed. Nothing in the atmosphere could be deadly, but . . . the holograms had not prepared Elara for this. They never took into account the way another planet might smell.

In the distance, Elara could see a second shuttle gliding across the horizon. In a few seconds it docked with Elara's shuttle, forming a two-car train.

"Who lives here?" Elara wondered aloud to herself. There were no signs of life anywhere.

Just then, a large procession of figures emerged from

the trees. At first Elara thought they were students. But as the figures got closer, she could see that these were robots—mindless lifter bots common on industrial planets. They were loading large and heavy boxes onto the shuttle. But there was still no student in sight . . .

Elara pressed the hatch button, opening the sealed connection between the two cars. With a few cautious steps, she was inside the new shuttle. The hatch slid quietly shut behind her. The familiar smell of Thui Prime surrounded her. But all she could see were boxes. Lots and lots of boxes.

"Hello?" Elara called out.

No response. Odd.

Elara walked more boldly now. There was no one on the shuttle. Just her and some cargo.

"But where's the student?" Elara muttered to herself. "If this is all their stuff, where are they?"

With a lurch, the two connected shuttles launched back into the sky. Elara steadied herself against a large box as the transport picked up speed. But something about this box was not like the others. For one thing, it was yellow and . . . squishy. What kind of species brought a large, squishy, sponge from a super-smelly planet to school?

There was a small white name tag attached to the yellow item. With a glance, Elara quickly read the name.

"Clare?"

Elara shook her head. Whoever Clare was, her luggage was weird. And she had definitely missed the transport. And STS had very strict attendance policies. Orientation would occur immediately after the shuttles docked.

Through the window, the stars began to streak, and the now-familiar colors of hyperspace filled her view. Elara sighed. Soon they'd reach another world. Hopefully then she'd get to meet some actual classmates.

CHAPTER 003

The loneliness didn't last long. Soon it was replaced by something else. Chaos.

The shuttle train had dropped onto several more fascinating worlds: a water planet with floating cities, a desert world with an underground population, and a jungle planet with more greenery than she'd ever seen in her life. With each stop, the train connected to more shuttles, loading up dozens of new students along the way.

The school shuttle train was now more than forty cars long and filled with all kinds of beings, species from planets Elara had never even heard of. Sure, there were lots of humans and humanoids, but there were also fluffy yellow-and-green kids with gills, translucent crystalline students, and a kid who looked like he might actually be a living shadow. It was amazing and wonderful and exactly what Elara had always hoped it would be like to leave her farming community.

"Excuse me . . . ," Elara said as she pushed through the crowded vehicle. She had made the mistake of leaving her seat to explore, and the vacant spot was now filled with students. There wasn't much to do but walk farther down the line until she found an open seat.

"So . . . uh . . . hi. Can I sit here?" Elara said, pointing to an open chair between four other first-years toward the front.

The girl on Elara's left looked up briefly, nodding a slight hello before turning away. The three others— all boys—were laughing among themselves, staring at a pocket holo-game. No one seemed particularly interested in the new girl. *This is part of it*, Elara thought. *Can't be intimidated on the first day.*

"My name's Elara," she added boldly. "From Vega Antilles. Sector 17."

One of the boys seemed to finally notice Elara—a Tharndarian with large eyes and no hair. "I'm Peter. These two are Silent Dave and Scrubby. Well . . ." He looked at the one identified as Scrubby, a larger boy with golden skin. Elara wasn't familiar with his species. "His name's actually Steve. But he likes to be called Scrubby."

Scrubby looked up, pointing a thumb at himself and nodding. "Scrubby's a good name. Gonna be famous one day. Gotta have a good name if you wanna be famous."

"Sure," Elara said, without being sure at all. "Good names are . . . important? You . . . uh . . . What do you plan to do to make yourself famous?"

"Dunno," Scrubby replied. "Come up with some killer world designs that break some records. Maybe solve the 'Impossible Equation' or invent a species no one ever thought of. That sort of thing."

"I mean . . . which branch of terraforming are you planning on studying?"

The girl to Elara's left looked up again, rolling her eyes. "We're all first-years. It's general ed. Don't you know that?"

"Well, yeah. But I mean, you think about it, right?"

"*Pff,*" the girl said, turning away.

"Ah, don't mind her," Peter said. "That's Suue

Damo'n. She's the very best of everything ever. Just ask her, and she'll make sure you know."

Suue glared at Peter. Elara decided it was best to ignore Suue's attitude and talk to the boys instead. "I'm hoping to be a bioengineer and work with microorganisms and animals."

Peter shrugged. "Probably geology, I guess. That's what my parents think, anyway. Every planet has rocks."

"An artist," Suue suddenly interjected. "I'm going to be an artist. I'll be designing worlds, leading and shaping the aesthetic of our galaxy. You'll see."

Elara looked at Suue with surprise, the words flooding out of her mouth without thinking. "But no one is really ever 'just' an artist. You become a world designer because of your work in your field. You still have to have a specialty."

Suue frowned at Elara. "Really? Like I don't know that? I'm a math expert. The highest level of art in the galaxy is math, and I can use that to work in any field I want. That's how it works when you're good at math."

"There's more to terraforming than just math," Elara answered. She was feeling a little defensive now. She had studied planetary art her entire life. "Every world designer has a foundation . . . like Mik Sigliain. Everyone knows his planets or his work in the Auureie

Cluster. But he was still a zoologist for twenty years beforehand. Or Pabs Higdaldoo. He worked as a botanist before he designed—"

Suue waved her hand in Elara's face. "Who cares! Just because they had to take other jobs to prove themselves doesn't mean everyone has to! I have a vision, an artistic vision."

"Okay. Sorry. I just . . . I'm sure you have a plan. Okay?"

The room fell awkwardly silent for several minutes. Outside, the colors of the warp tunnel had shifted from green to blue. The train was accelerating and streaking past the stars faster and faster. Blue shift, they called it. A phenomenon of light that changes the color of an object based on how far away it is.

Scrubby and Peter were looking at another holo-game. Silent Dave was reading something. Elara was just about to make another stab at conversation when Suue spoke.

"Why are you here?"

Elara felt her stomach lurch. "Well, um . . . terraforming school. I think we kinda covered that."

"But look at you," Suue continued, looking at Elara like a bug under a microscope. "You're, what, like some kind of farm girl? From the outer rim of nowhere anyone's ever heard of? You have to be someone if you want to get anywhere in terraforming. You have to have real skills."

Elara felt her cheeks flush. "I won a scholarship. I know a lot about terraforming . . ."

"Is that why they stuck you back in the cargo shuttles? Or did you just sneak on board and hope that no one would notice that you clearly don't belong here."

Peter looked up from his game. "Hey, Suue. Come on."

"I'm just saying what you're thinking, and you know it." Suue turned back on Elara, who was, for the first time, speechless. "I'm not trying to be mean, but you have no idea what you're in for. My family owns a planet. I was literally bioengineered to be a mathematical genius. I'm like a living computer, and you sit down next to me with your big eyes and spout off your little dreams and think you're in the same league? Do yourself a favor and go right back home. It's where you belong."

Elara looked up, really seeing the crowd around her for the first time. Their perfectly pressed clothes. Their expensive rings. Smooth skin that had never been burned by a day working under the sun.

Even Silent Dave was staring at her now. Suue looked smug, Scrubby looked embarrassed, and Peter looked like he desperately wanted to be somewhere else. The three boys had seemed nice enough. They weren't agreeing with anything that Suue had said . . .

. . . but they weren't disagreeing with it, either.

Elara stood up, grabbed her backpack, and walked out of the cabin without another word.

It was frustrating but hardly a surprise. At home or in remote corners of the galaxy, kids were still kids. Elara pushed through the crowd, her frustration mounting as she bumped past her new classmates.

Tired of asking for permission, Elara spotted an open seat and took it, suddenly not caring what anyone thought. She had worked hard to get where she was. She wasn't about to be scared off by anyone.

Looking up, she realized there was only one other person in the compartment. An unusually large person who filled every inch of space in the train car.

Elara blinked, unsure of what to say. It wasn't just the unusual size of the being. It was that the student was seemingly made of stone, with eyes that looked like burning coals. Eyes that were suddenly staring at Elara.

The scary giant reached out a hand, each one of its fingers nearly as wide as Elara's entire body. With a flare of energy behind its sinister eyes, the creature smiled and said, in a high-pitched, squeaky voice, "Hi! My name's Knot!"

Knot reached down and produced the tiniest, daintiest pot of tea that Elara had ever seen, pouring it into a frilly, floral-printed cup. Handing Elara the tiny cup, the stone creature spoke once more, smiling the goofiest, most disarming smile a giant stone creature could manage.

"Would you like some tea?"

CHAPTER 004

The rest of the journey was much improved.

Elara discovered that Knot was a lovely hostess. Absolutely charming. She was a young Grix from planet Grixicon in Sector 32—about as far away from Elara's home in Sector 17 as you could travel without hitting unexplored space. Knot was planning on studying atmospheric manipulations.

"I've always liked things light and fluffy, like clouds. I used to stare at them all day." Knot sipped her tea, while Elara helped herself to a third tiny lemon cake. "I figured why not study weather? Then it's like looking at the clouds all the time, you know?"

"Mmf," said Elara, her mouth filled with cake. "Hmmpfh," she added happily.

Outside, the stars had shifted back to green and were now well on their way to the final red shift that signaled the end of the long journey. The shuttle had added another two dozen cars by this point, and excited students rushed up and down the main hall of the train.

Elara hadn't bothered stepping back out of the compartment. Knot was perfectly happy for the company and outraged when Elara opened up about her experience with Suue.

"Nonsense," Knot said, finishing her cup. "You belong here just as much as anyone. Probably even more than them. You had to work your way here without any help. Besides, no reason for people to be rude. I mean, I get that we're all strangers. But to be so cliquish on the first day?" The Grix daintily waved her massive slab of a hand in disgust. "Ugh. I have no patience for it!"

"I was just feeling a little overwhelmed," Elara responded. "I've never been off-planet before. Until today, I never met someone who wasn't a farmer or related to a farmer."

Knot poured another tiny cup of tea, emptying the pot as she did. "And you met a bunch of snobby people on your first day out. Their loss, I'd say!"

Elara felt uncomfortable for a moment. "In all fairness, maybe I'm just as bad as them. When I first saw you, I thought . . . Well . . . I was nervous. I've never met anyone . . ."

"So gigantic and monster-like?" Knot said with an amused smile.

Elara felt her ears burn with shame. "I'm so sorry! I was just surprised, and . . . I know I need to not be prejudiced, but . . ."

"You saw me and thought I was a giant, scary monster." With a massive shrug, Knot brushed off Elara's protests. "It's no big deal."

"It . . . isn't?" Elara was thoroughly confused. "Why isn't it?"

"Well, because technically I am a giant scary monster." Knot smiled. "On my world, the Grix are a savage race that terrorize the innocent and haunt the night."

Knot took a bite of lemon cake before continuing.

"The Kix—they're kinda-sorta like you, only smaller with a few more arms—they tell stories to their children about the Grix. Scary tales of how we like to eat them. You know the kind, I'm sure."

"But . . . you're not a monster. You're really sweet. You gave me tea. And cakes!"

Knot sighed. "I know. I'm a terrible disappointment to my family. They howled and snarled every time I talked about the beautiful clouds and raindrops. They wanted to make a proper monster out of me, force me to give up my dreams. 'Terrorize just one village!' they would beg. 'You'll see how much you like it!' they would say . . ."

Outside, the shuttle train began its final descent.

"Oh, look!" Knot said in her twinkly fairy voice as her massive hands clapped together. "We're landing! I can't wait! We're going to have such fun times!"

Elara looked out the window and saw that the ship had dropped out of hyperspace. Below she could see a planet—a beautiful, massive gem of a planet, home to the Seven Systems School of Terraforming: Paragon.

CHAPTER 005

lara couldn't focus on anything else. The multihued world was more beautiful than any hologram or picture she had ever seen.

The long string of shuttles landed just as the warm orange sun peeked over the distant mountains of translucent crystal. An enormous prism projected a rainbow across the landscape. Every student aboard the train pressed themselves against the window to see the spectacular sunrise on the world they would soon be calling home.

Once they had landed, Elara grabbed her bag and pushed her way toward one of the train's exits. She was finally about to step onto a new world. A proper new world this time, unlike that smelly swamp one she was already trying to forget. Knot followed behind her, surprisingly quiet in her footsteps. It took several minutes for every student to reach the door—though the path opened up a bit when Elara's future classmates noticed the massive stone giant.

The train let the students off on a large, hovering, covered platform that looked like it was carved from an impossibly massive seashell. Except it wasn't impossible. Not at all. Not on Paragon.

"It's called the Brobdingnagian Buttercup," Elara whispered excitedly to Knot. "It was bioengineered way back when the planet was first terraformed. This isn't even as large as they grow!"

"And look!" she continued as she bumped her way past students. "You can see the ocean!" It was true. Through the semitransparent platform, they could see the watery depths below. The sea here was purple in color, deep and rich, with a crystalline quality.

She squinted. There were shapes in the water. Large and fast silhouettes swimming rapidly back and forth. She was about to point it out to Knot, when she realized that no one was moving anymore. Instead, all three hundred first-year students were staring straight into the air. And with a glance, Elara suddenly forgot all about the ocean and the train station.

High above them were the famous jellies of Paragon—vast floating animals with sweeping tendrils drifting lazily down. Each one was at least a hundred feet wide, though most of that was air. They were like living soap bubbles, each one a different variety of dancing pastel colors.

The docile jellies drifted far, far above in the bright sky, absorbing sunlight and refracting it, adding to the kaleidoscopic rainbow effect that was beaming all around the children.

Everything here was beautiful. Impossibly and perfectly beautiful.

It was exactly as Elara had always read. Paragon was the most beautiful planet ever conceived, designed and constructed by the most brilliant and artistic terraformers ever known. From the soft orange grass to the dense forest of onyx trees. In foliage, silicate- and carbon-based life blended seamlessly to form soft crystalline patterns. Closing your eyes, you could hear the distant sounds of woodland animals.

And the air! The air smelled just like freshly baked cookies. *How was that even possible?* Elara thought.

She quickly decided that, at least for the moment, the "how" didn't matter.

This was it. This was a terraformed world. The peak of beauty and height of function. A world that took the very best of nature and somehow made something more out of it.

"Students. Your attention, please."

The voice was soft, yet it cut through the crowd like a knife. Floating above the round platform was a large glowing head. The hologram belonged to a member of the furry and catlike Rakeesta species. Elara recognized the woman immediately, and judging by the awestruck reaction of her classmates, so did everyone else. This was Headmistress Kyrsten Nebulina, winner of the Diamond Dragon Award, three-time holder of the Omnitarian Award of Universal Altruism, member of the Council of Affiliated Worlds, and writer of the most infamous piece of terraforming lore—the so-called Impossible Equation.

"I am Headmistress Nebulina," she said, her voice carrying a slight purr. "Welcome, class of galactic year 09.BQ.92. It is my great pleasure to escort you all to your new home, our school—the Seven Systems School of Terraforming Sciences and Arts."

A round of applause broke out among the crowd as the students stepped off the hovering platform and down a long and winding path. It was a wide road, and Elara found herself in the middle of the sea of students, unable to get a look at any of the vegetation.

A moment later she no longer cared. The path turned, and there it was: The school itself, a series of gleaming spires of marble and crystal, intertwined with massive organic buildings. Living trees blossomed into towering structures, all erupting from a surface of natural topaz.

Headmistress Nebulina addressed the crowd of first-year students as they proceeded toward the school grounds.

"Your first few days here will undoubtedly be ones of exploration, as I understand that for many of you, this journey has been long. However, there are some very important rules you all must understand."

"One: You will not leave the campus without supervision. This is a strictly enforced rule, and failure to obey this rule will result in expulsion." All the students seemed to take this very seriously, and Elara noticed the crowd grow quiet.

"Two: You will not utilize terraforming techniques or technologies without the express permission of an instructor."

This rule seemed to be met with less importance, and Elara expected it would be broken quickly. She wouldn't blame anyone personally. How could they not explore the skills they were being trained in?

"Three," Nebulina continued. "Remember our school pledge. Recite it every day. It is the principal foundation by which all terraforming should be governed. It's brief, and you can all learn it right now. Three simple words."

Nebulina raised a furry hand, and a large glimmering holo-projection floated in the sky next to the headmistress. The air was emblazoned in electric blue letters.

"Do no harm," the headmistress recited.

"Think about these words. Do no harm," she repeated. "In terraforming, the power over life is in your hands. Every plant, every micro-cellular life-form, they are your responsibility. It is not enough to build new planets. We must make planets responsibly."

Elara and everyone else nodded obediently.

"Now, students, in a moment we will reach the gates of the school. There you will be scanned and you will receive your schedules. Your accommodations have already been prepared, so you will be directed to the dormitories. Take these next two days to familiarize yourself with both campus and curriculum. Rest. Relax. And make yourself ready."

With a wink and a smile, the giant, glimmering

head of the Rakeesta concluded the orientation. "Remember, students," she said with a wry smile, "your journey begins . . . now!"

And with that, the holographic head vanished, and behind it stood the massive gates of the school. Below, the road the children had been walking on was now composed of a radiant, alien crystal. It led to a set of wide obsidian steps that ended at the school's administrative building.

With a lurch, the massive gates swung open wide. Elara smiled and started to climb.

CHAPTER 006

After being scanned into the campus student tracking system and receiving her school communicator, Elara was officially ready to begin her first year.

Like most other students, Elara and Knot began by flipping through their communicators to find out their class schedules and dorm room assignments. The device folded over like a clamshell, with a soft and flexible screen inside.

"Dorm assignments are up, but no class schedules still," Elara groaned, reading from the small screen.

"I guess we'll have to wait!" the Grix said pleasantly.

The girls were walking through the glass skywalk that led to one of the first-year dormitories. At first they thought the path would curve around a large oak tree. Instead, the walkway opened up inside the tree itself. Living wood shaped a giant spiral staircase inside the tree's trunk. It was at least thirty feet wide and lit with a cascading rainbow of naturally bioluminescent floating seed pods.

As the girls climbed, the stairs led to a massive common room inside the tree's canopy. This was their dormitory, high up in the clouds, capable of housing more than two hundred newly enrolled students.

After a few awestruck moments, Knot and Elara pushed their way into the small throng of equally impressed first-year students.

"Compartment 313B," Elara read from her communicator. "And my roommates are named Beezle and . . . Clare? I think I saw her stuff on the train . . ."

"312A!" Knot exclaimed with a gravelly grin. "We're neighbors!"

"That's fantastic!" Elara said. "Who are you rooming with?"

Knot gave a sympathetic smile. "I'm so sorry, sweetie, but I'm in a single unit. The doors will auto-lock me in so I don't . . . wander."

Elara gave Knot a curious look. "Locked in? Why?"

"It's a Grix thing. We're heavy sleepers, and we occasionally . . ." Knot shrugged and looked embarrassed. "Well . . . we wander while in a dream state, seeking . . . late-night snacks. We're naturally a hunter species, mostly small mammals give or take"— Knot held out a hand, holding it roughly Elara's height—"about so big. Anyway . . . it really is best that I have my own space. You understand, right?"

Elara nodded very quickly in response. Then, sighing, she looked out at the crowd of freshmen. "Anyway . . . I hope *my* roommates are nice. I'm not so great at making friends."

Knot gave the sulking girl a friendly punch on the arm, which sent Elara staggering several feet. "Of course they'll be nice! You're just shy. Making friends is much easier than you think. Here, let me show you . . ." And with that, the Grix disappeared into the crowd of students nearby.

Elara rubbed her bruised arm. She had been so quick to judge Knot's appearance. A lifetime of isolation on a faraway farm world had left her very . . .

But Elara never finished the thought. Instead,

the Grix stomped back across the common room, grasping a thin young girl with a bald head and light blue skin.

Knot dropped the new student at Elara's feet. "Here you go, Elara!" Knot said happily, pointing to the girl. "I found you a new friend!"

Surprisingly, the girl Knot grabbed didn't run away.

"I am Beezle," the girl said cautiously, rising to her feet. She was a pleasant girl with a half smile on her face. It was as if she existed in a permanent state of calm. "From the Arctuiaan settlement in the Delta region of Quasi-Space."

"Oh!" Elara perked up. "Beezle! What a weird coincidence! I think we're roommates!"

"What are the odds?" Knot said with a guilty smile. "You'd almost think I peeked at the public dorm profile listings."

"I'm Elara. And I've heard of Arctuiaans!" Elara continued, suddenly excited. "You have, like, some kind of hive mind. Right? Like bees?"

The girl turned a slightly darker shade of blue. "Well . . . it's not quite like that. When we sleep, we rejoin the OverMind. It's um . . . it's kind of like a hive mind? More like thought sharing, if that makes sense?"

"It completely makes sense," Knot said, elbowing Elara. "My friend didn't mean to be rude. She just left the farm. This is all so new to her."

Elara raised an eyebrow. "I can still hear you, Knot. Besides, you're the one who walked up and kidnapped the poor girl."

"It's okay." The Arctuiaan smiled lightly. "I really don't mind talking about it. Or the kidnapping, I guess. Though that was very weird. Anyway, I'm excited to room with you, Elara! It's all so strange. You are the first beings I have met that have never communed with the OverMind. It must be very . . ." The girl looked thoughtful, searching for the right word. "Lonely. Yes. It must be lonely and quiet when you sleep."

"I guess?" Elara responded. "I'm usually not aware. And quiet is preferable for humans at rest. I—"

There was a buzzing noise, and Elara pulled out her personal comm system. Opening up the device, Elara saw a message from the school. "Hey, guys . . . they just released class schedules!"

Knot and Beezle instantly grabbed their own communicators. Beezle let out a loud and happy gasp. "I have been selected to attend Dr. Amiba's course on magnetic core stabilization! And I'm enrolled in Seismic Studies! I registered for the course late and was uncertain there would be room!"

Elara quickly flipped through her schedule. "What time do you have Seismic? I'm on the third period with Mr. Trutton . . ."

Knot was quick to jump in. "I have Trutton's class, too! With a follow-up course in flora design." The Grix looked up. "I didn't think that was even offered to first-years."

Beezle smiled. "And I have it, too! We are all on the same course schedule! As friends should be!"

Elara's jaw dropped as she looked from Knot to Beezle. "We're friends? For real? I mean, we kind of forced you to hang out with us—"

Beezle shook her head vehemently. "No. At first that was true. But I have decided that now we are an alliance, and by the code of my people, I shall honor our newly forged bonds!"

Elara opened her mouth to respond, when suddenly the conversation was interrupted by a loud bell.

Older students, ones who had been attending the school for some time, immediately began to move. Uncertain of what was happening, Elara called out to a passing Deltaainian, "Hey! What's that bell? Where's everyone going?"

The amphibious upperclassman grinned with both of his mouths. "That's the first warning to check in to your bunks, freshmen. You gotta head up to your rooms."

Elara turned back to her two new friends. "Well?" she said. "Shall we check out our new home?"

CHAPTER 007

A familiar large and yellow rectangle propped open the door of Compartment 313B.

"Oh!" Beezle said to the rectangle. "You must be Clare. Hello! I am Beezle! From the Arctuiaan settlement in the Delta region of Quasi-Space. I am not like a bee, though I can understand how my name might cause some minor confusions."

"Um. Beezle?" Elara interrupted.

"I am so rude!" Beezle blushed. "Clare, these are my

friends—Elara Adele Vaughn, of Vega Antilles V, and Knot, of the Grix. Elara is also staying in this room."

"This is cargo," Elara pointed out. "I saw this in the shuttle, stacked with a bunch of boxes. It's not . . ." Elara looked at the large yellow sponge. Tentatively, she reached out and poked at the soft rectangle that couldn't possibly be a living being. ". . . My roommate?"

"Elara! You really must not judge! Why, this yellow rectangle will be living with you, and you must be respectful!" Knot chastised.

Clare, in response, said nothing. She also did nothing. She was, as far as Elara could tell, completely devoid of sentience.

"It is so good to meet you!" exclaimed Beezle.

"Well," Knot added with a shrug. "I'm going to check in to my room. Toodle-oo, neighbors!"

Elara waved goodbye to her new friend as she searched for the right words for her unusual roommate. "Hi. Um. Clare. How's . . ." She looked around. The door slowly creaked, held in place by the motionless yellow slab. "How's things?"

There was no response.

"So . . . ?" Elara asked.

"I do not believe she can hear. Or speak. Or move," Beezle said. "She is in her dormant state."

"So how is she going to go to class? Or learn

anything?" Elara pointed out.

"I am under the impression that Clare is a Blossh. Her species slowly absorbs information from those they are near. How exciting! Our information will be absorbed!"

"Sure. Great. That's just what I hoped for when I signed up." Elara flopped down on her bunk. "I can study, and she can absorb what I study."

"Aw," Beezle said. "I think Clare now feels sad."

"Sorry if I made you feel bad, Clare. You are welcome to my . . . knowledge. I guess," Elara said, addressing the slab. "Why not?"

Elara slumped down on the bed, amazed at just how tired she was. She could use a quick nap before dinner. Beezle carefully unpropped the door and gently leaned Clare against a wall.

"Well, anyway. I'm glad you're rooming with me, Beezle." Elara hesitated. "It's been . . . a difficult day. I left my one real friend behind for a completely new world. It means a lot to meet you and Knot."

Beezle blinked, clearly waiting for Elara to say more.

"And Clare," Elara added. "Good to meet all three of you. Really."

Beezle smiled as she slipped a thin metal ring around her head. "Yes, friend Elara. I do understand the difficulties of leaving one's home. New experiences are both wonderful and frightening. Why," she continued, "I endured the hallucination waverider as part of my journey through Quasi-Space. It was like unending torment." Beezle then paused. "Well, it was like that until it ended. Then it was pretty much fine."

"Right." Elara said. "Your day might have been rougher than mine."

The two girls started to unpack their belongings. Elara fired off a quick message to Danny, explaining little bits of the day and promising to return his call. Beezle activated the ring around her head and joined the OverMind. This meant sitting upright and mumbling to herself in a strange language with her eyes wide open.

The old Elara would have been disturbed, maybe even a little scared. But this? This was . . . exciting. She had made it to the school of her dreams. And she had two—*three*—new friends. Very unusual friends, but that was what made the galaxy interesting. Unusual and exciting new cultures, all coming together and discovering that, at the core, they really weren't very different. They weren't scary. They weren't weird. They were all just people.

That was the moment when Beezle opened her mouth wide. With what sounded like a howl, the girl thrashed around for a moment and stood up on her bed. Then her head turned sideways in a move that was possible for the Arctuiaan but was kind of terrifying from a human perspective, and Beezle began to speak with a deep voice that did not belong to her.

"BEWARE."

Elara felt her skin grow cold. "Beezle?"

Beezle reached out, and Elara felt a hand come to rest on her shoulder. But when she looked her new friend in the eyes, it was clear that Beezle was not in the driver's seat.

"BEWARE, ELARA, BEWARE. THE EMPIRE THAT DID NOT CARE." The strange deep voice grew louder. "THEY WERE LOST. LOST, AND THEIR SPIRITS DO ROAM. IN SEARCH OF A NEW, ETERNAL HOME."

Elara shook her friend. "Beezle! Hey! Snap out of it!"

Beezle's eyes rolled into her head, and her fingers curled like claws. Her whole body tensed, and then, much to Elara's confusion, she lay back down and began snoring.

Clearly freaked out, Elara poked Beezle with a pencil.

"Oh!" Beezle said, her voice happy as ever. "Is it morning? Shall we rush off to begin our exciting day?

"No," Elara said firmly. "No, you just started

channeling some scary voodoo monster and said that there was some empire looking for a home."

Beezle sat up. "Ah! You were graced by a visit from the OverMind!"

"I was *what* now?"

"The OverMind! All my people's subconscious thought manifested as a singular consciousness. How lucky you are for such a visit. It is quite rare that they appear to one so soon after meeting!"

"But it sounded so . . ."

"Dark and bleak and hopeless?"

"Yes."

"Filled with vaguely prophetic-sounding sinister storybook rhymes?"

"I guess so. Maybe?"

"Hmm . . . ," Beezle answered, looking thoughtful. "Definitely the OverMind, then. It leans on the pessimistic side. A by-product of being all-knowing and omniscient."

And then the small and sweet blue girl sat back down on the bed, and the half smile returned to her face, completely carefree. Nearby, the yellow rectangle that was Clare did nothing. Beezle closed her eyes and gave a slight snoring sound, and about one compartment over, where Knot was housed, came sounds that could only be described as a bear chewing on a giant pile of gravel, followed by the sound of a door being pounded.

"Nope," Elara said to herself again. "Nothing weird or scary here. Not at all." And with that thought, she pulled the blanket over her head and proceeded to nap before dinner.

CHAPTER 008

Time passed faster at STS than Elara would have ever expected—faster than life on the farm world, at any rate. A new routine was formed pretty quickly. Early-morning classes were devoted to basic geology and the fundamentals of elemental research. Afternoon classes were divided between examining the basic building blocks of life and analyzing the mechanics of nuclear physics. It was all pretty basic at this stage, and Elara found the classes fun but not too challenging.

At the same time, Elara couldn't forget about Beezle's premonition from the first day. Almost everything uttered by the OverMind was generally considered nonsense, but it was stuck in Elara's mind, anyway. It just felt . . . important.

"They were . . . lost . . . ," she wrote down in her notebook, drawing a circle around the words.

Knot looked over her shoulder. "Elara!" she hissed. "Are you still worrying about that silly little poem? You need to pay attention to class! This is a pass/fail!"

The class in question was Theoretical Subatomic Studies—a basic introduction to manipulating matter on an atomic level. Turning one element into a completely different one.

"Ugh!" Elara whispered back. "But isn't it odd? If it's a poem or a song, I haven't been able to find any evidence . . ."

"Do you know I once heard a Glonopegane spider tell a joke?" Beezle added. "The galaxy is a strange and mysterious place that rarely has any deeper meaning. It's easier to stop looking for one."

Elara slammed the notebook shut, feeling a bit grumpy that her friends weren't as interested in getting to the heart of this mystery. "Fine," she said. "I'll leave it alone!"

"Good! Now, can we please pay attention?" Knot said in a rather gravelly voice. "I mean, you could talk about this freely in maybe twenty minutes when class is over, you know?"

Elara started to respond, when a shadow fell over her. Elara, Beezle, and Knot looked up in unison and saw the scowling face of the professor looming above them.

"Your attention, ladies."

The girls slouched deeply in their seats. Catching the attention of Professor Thur'uer had long since proven to be a bad idea. Students who had fallen on the reptilian teacher's bad side were rumored to have been quarantined in the Zone of Endings.

Elara gulped. It was probably all lies. But still . . .

"I'm certain you must be whispering about very important matters," the professor hissed. "Perhaps you are so excited about today's lesson that you cannot contain yourselves? Is that it?"

The girls managed to look sheepish, with Beezle's blue skin pulsating a very dark shade that, as Elara had come to understand, meant deep embarrassment.

"Well, since that's the case, I think I can make your lives more interesting." Professor Thur'uer's forked tongue slithered in and out quickly, testing the air, taking in the scent of her prey. The students were afraid, and Elara knew that the teacher could sense it. "Please come to the front of the class and display your skills for us all to see. Prove to me that I should not expel you from my class."

Knot shot Elara a quick irritated glance, but it was too late. All three girls stood up and made their way down the stairs to the classroom floor.

The class was set up in the style of a small amphitheater, with a large circular platform built at ground level and seats swelling up around all sides. On the podium there was a large table, complete with an intricate series of plastic and glass laboratory equipment all connected to a large computer system.

"Since it's obvious that you know so much about bio-atomic manipulation, I think it only appropriate that you provide a demonstration for the entire class." The teacher picked up a test tube filled with pale orange algae. "This strain of algae is known to have some very interesting properties. Depending on the chemicals introduced, a wide variety of reactions are possible. Some good . . . some less than good. But all involve a manipulation of the basic atomic formula."

The professor slid the test tube into a centrifugal vortex, spinning the tube rapidly and separating the chemical components of the algae. With a quick flip of her wrist, she ejected the tube and tossed it to Elara.

Elara looked at the tube. "Why is the algae glowing?" she asked.

Before anyone could answer, the orange glowing goop bubbled over and spilled onto the floor. Elara jumped back, and Knot cringed. Beezle was less alarmed and instead made a soft purring noise from the back of her throat.

"Ah. I see that perhaps you three did not pay as much attention to my lecture as I had hoped. You see, when agitated, the molecular composition of this substance breaks down and becomes unstable. Any minute now, the algae could reach a critical point of instability and fill this classroom with a fast-acting toxin." She gestured toward a large table crowded with an overwhelming number of potions and powders. "The neutralizing agent can be found in that array of chemicals on the work desk. Good luck."

And with that, the professor stepped backward off the platform and snapped a transparent energy shield into place, trapping Elara, Knot, and Beezle in with the glowing algae.

"Hey!" Elara yelled, hammering her fist on the energy shield. "You can't just lock us up with this! It's dangerous!"

The professor didn't flinch. "Dangerous? You are training to be terraformers! Risk is part of the equation. Do you think all science will be performed under ideal conditions? That you will have time and resources abundant?"

The professor turned and looked at the collective classroom. "On that note, how much time do we have, class?"

The entire class answered in unison, "Two minutes, Professor Thur'uer!"

Professor Thur'uer turned her serpentine countenance back toward the intimidated trio. Elara felt tiny beads of sweat appear on her brow, while Beezle's color was shifting to a previously unseen blue green.

"Two minutes," Professor Thur'uer said. "The clock is ticking. But don't worry. This toxin won't harm you. It will simply affect your taste buds for a week. I do hope you like the flavor of Zebroniazin stinkweed. It will become very familiar very soon."

With one last glance at the bubbling angry mass of growing algae, the girls grabbed vials of bio-liquids and went to work.

"Use the lattice inducer," whispered Knot. "It should slow the chemical reaction!"

"But what about using a neutralizing acid?" Beezle responded as she searched frantically through the various tubes and vials.

"It's not a base element!" Knot growled. "You have to stop the cellular reaction first!"

Elara scanned the tabletop. Powders and chemicals and gels and all sorts of things were strewn about, and any one of them might stop the out-of-control algae . . . or just as easily create a reaction that could level the building. Chemistry . . . chemicals . . . Elara had studied the basics of bio-manipulations since she was a baby. It was standard curriculum across the galaxy. But this . . . this was a real test. And it was all related to atomic conversion . . .

Elara slapped her forehead. "Listen! We don't need to stop the algae from destabilizing! We can accelerate the atoms instead!"

"And achieve what? A massive explosion?!" Knot yelled.

"We can contain the explosion with the force field!" Beezle said.

"Oh, sure." Knot shrugged. "I mean, it's not like we're INSIDE THE FORCE FIELD!"

"Thirty seconds," Professor Thur'uer said with a grin. "Perhaps none of you are ready for such advanced education."

Desperate, Elara looked for something to solve the problem. That's when she noticed the large computer. The one that had emerged from the floor. The machine was a standard system you'd find in a school of this nature, designed to analyze and synthesize complex chemical components. They were also used in farming worlds when you needed to increase or decrease nitrogen and oxygen levels in the soil.

This all occurred to Elara in the flash of a second. "Beezle!" she yelled as she grabbed one of the computer conduits, ripping it from its housing in a shower of sparks. "Reroute the computer systems to produce a continuous feedback loop!"

"What? What are you doing?!" Professor Thur'uer said with a screech. "Stop that! You're destroying school equipment!"

"Hey!" Elara shouted. "You said we had to solve this? So we're going to solve it!"

Beezle looked up from the conduit she was grabbing. "Ah! I see. So this will induce an atomic fission event!"

Professor Thur'uer's green skin went decidedly pale. "Wait. What? You can't do that!"

With that said, Elara slammed the sparking conduit into the growing pile of smelly algae, shooting an electric current through the orange-and-green slime. With an explosive flash, everyone in the room was knocked off their feet, temporarily blinded by the bright flare.

As the smoke cleared, Elara picked herself up.

The algae was gone. The computer was destroyed, overloaded with an infinite feedback loop.

Professor Thur'uer looked at the result, flabbergasted. In the center of the podium, floating about seven feet in the air, was a brightly glowing orb. "What . . . what did you do?" she said, the snarky hiss now gone from her voice.

"A star," Elara said as she looked at the orange-and-green ball of energy. "We made a star."

CHAPTER 009

Unsurprisingly, the three girls soon found themselves in the office of Headmistress Nebulina.

"Reckless!" Professor Thur'uer was yelling. "Disrespectful! In complete violation of every classroom ordinance! These three . . . three hooligans have no thought or consideration for the ethics of atomic manipulation! Or for the safety of the classroom!"

The headmistress's office was spacious but sparsely decorated. Situated at the center of campus, above the shuttle hangar, there were several doors leading out to various passageways. There was a white desk with a small keyboard built into it and a holographic monitor floating in place. On the wall behind the headmistress's desk was a painting of a gigantic whirlpool in space. Other than a few chairs for visitors—also stark white—there was only one other object in the room: a large bronze plaque, probably at least seven feet tall, with a complex equation engraved on it. This was Headmistress Nebulina's Impossible Equation—a groundbreaking theory proving that instant terraforming is dangerous and impossible. Covered in dents and scratches, it had traveled far and wide over the many years since it had been created.

Elara felt a quick buzz from her communicator. With a glance, she realized she was going to miss another call from Danny. But there was nothing she could do about it now.

Looking at Professor Thur'uer, Headmistress Nebulina tilted her head in a feline manner, the catlike aspects of her features exaggerated in the pose. "Professor," she asked in a quiet voice, "let me ask you this, just so I understand correctly. Did the children engage in reckless behavior before or after you unleashed a potentially destructive agent in the middle of a classroom of first-year students?"

"Ah," Professor Thur'uer said with a soft hiss. "Um," she added, suddenly caught off guard. "You see . . . that . . . that was . . . different . . ."

"Yes," Headmistress Nebulina replied. "I look forward to your detailed report. In the meantime, I think I can manage these apparent 'hooligans.' You may return to your classroom."

Professor Thur'uer looked uncertain. "But . . . but it has a tiny sun spinning in the center of it now."

Headmistress Nebulina pressed a button on her desk. "M'rell? Could you send a cleanup crew to the biosphere building? Tell them to bring a containment tube. They'll know what to do when they get there."

"Right away, Headmistress," returned an efficient-sounding voice.

"There we go." The headmistress smiled after logging off the communications system. "I'll have that delivered to the observatory. In the meantime, Professor, I suggest you let this new star's light illuminate you as to the proper classroom etiquette of a teacher. Good day."

The professor slinked away, leaving Elara, Knot, and Beezle alone with Nebulina.

"So . . . ," the headmistress purred, appraising the

three students. "I think I know exactly what to do with the three of you."

"I assume you three are familiar with the foundation of our science?" Headmistress Nebulina said as she led the three students across the campus to a zoned-off section of the school. "Do no harm?"

All three girls nodded solemnly, each one fairly certain that this was the moment they would all be expelled. *At least the three new friends will all be together*, Elara thought glumly. Knot grumbled something savage and unintelligible in her native Grixian, and Elara reconsidered. Maybe a little alone time in the face of expulsion might be a good idea.

"Do you three know why we say, 'Do no harm'?" the headmistress continued.

Not waiting for the students to speak up, the headmistress answered her own question. "The fate of the Frils. And the abrupt end of the First Galactic War."

The headmistress reached a large round building made of crystal. Light shone through it, refracting a thousand times into the most amazing rainbow patterns. But what was inside was impossible to detect. With a quick press of her hand against a datalock, the door slid open, and inside . . . Elara gasped.

Inside was the galaxy.

The group walked inside. Beezle looked down. And quickly looked back up again. Below the feet of the children there was nothing but infinite space, stretching down as far as the eye could see. Knot swayed slightly, leaning on Elara for balance. It wasn't the most comfortable thing in the world, but Elara managed to keep from collapsing.

Typing on a control panel, the headmistress commanded a series of steps to materialize, a slow spiral staircase that extended up into the whirling sea of stars above. The entire thing was a hologram, of course. But the degree of realism created was like nothing the girls had ever seen.

The headmistress began climbing the steps. "Now, of course, I know you're aware of basic galactic history. But let's review, just for a moment."

The stairs stopped abruptly on a wide platform that appeared to float in the middle of whirling space. The headmistress waved a hand, and the stars and planets whirled by, as if the platform was flying to a new destination far, far away in the galaxy.

"Over a thousand years ago," the headmistress continued, "the seven sectors of populated space were at war with one another. It was a brutal time, when resources were scarce and our understanding of terraforming was comparatively limited."

Pointing a finger into the center of the known galaxy, the headmistress tapped a holographic planet, a large blue-and-orange world that looked both lush and vibrant. It was surrounded by two rings, each one spinning on a different axis so that the world resembled the icon of an atom.

"This was Frillianth—once a resource-rich world, one that the Frils exploited and burned until there was nothing left but rock and poison." The headmistress frowned as she continued. "The Frils believed it was their right to spread their rule across the galaxy. And so, they attempted to build a terraforming engine so powerful it could erase all life on a planet in minutes. Replace any ecosystem with one of their own design, leaving a world only suitable for their own species."

"The Impossible Equation . . ." Elara whispered in response.

Headmistress Nebulina tapped the planet again, and the incredibly realistic image of the world began to shimmer.

Elara watched as the rings that circled Frillianth began to contract. And then suddenly, with an explosive force, the planet imploded. In its place was now a massive wormhole.

"The Fril science was flawed. And their terraforming machines would never be deployed. Seventy billion lives," the headmistress said, with a note of sadness. "The entire Fril species, gone. Just like that. And not just the warlike rulers, but the civilians . . . the scientists . . . everyone on the Frillianth home world. It was a tragedy that ended the war . . . held up as proof that there are limits to what can be done with science. Boundaries that we are now taught to respect."

The headmistress pushed a few bits of holographic light around. A ring of artificial satellites appeared in orbit around the wormhole—seven in total. "The Frils were gone, and with them, the secrets to their terraforming weapons. Because of the horror that had occurred, the remaining systems met and declared peace. The leaders of all the sentient beings agreed to pool their resources together to find ways to safely, though slowly, create new worlds. All in the hope that war would never be needed again. It was the beginning of our Galactic Affiliation, one whose core belief, 'Do no harm,' governs us still today."

The three students jumped abruptly as Nebulina clapped her hands together. A door in the void of space slid open with white light pouring out. She gestured, and the students filed obediently out of the beautiful, but disorienting, room into a long hallway.

"At this point, I imagine you three are curious as to why I am spending so much time reviewing basic galactic history with you? You're also wondering exactly what kind of trouble you're in? Correct?"

Knot glared at Beezle, still irritated that she had been dragged into trouble along with her friends. Beezle shuffled about uncomfortably, but Elara decided to speak.

"Headmistress Nebulina . . . in all fairness, we didn't do anything wrong. I mean, we weren't paying as much attention as we should have, but Professor Thur'uer asked us to stop the growth of algae. She didn't say how we had to stop it."

The headmistress's yellow eyes narrowed. "I would think contextually, since you were in a bioengineering class focusing on the manipulations of organic elements through chemical stimuli, the solution would be one that fits the curriculum. Am I correct? Or do you really think your approach was appropriate?"

All three students shook their heads rapidly.

"Good," the headmistress said, staring all three students in the face. "At this school, creative solutions are always encouraged. But they must be tempered with experience and responsibility. To that end, you must be educated."

They group passed through another door, and

they soon found themselves in a large and cluttered warehouse. Towering shelves were strewn about in a disorganized fashion, each one covered with odd pieces of machinery. The walls were painted . . . sort of. Elara squinted and realized that there were layers and layers of graffiti covering the walls, equations and messages painted haphazardly, as if people had been using spray paint to jot down idle thoughts. At various workstations, groups of students were hard at work. Some of them were welding together large and mysterious machines. Another group was performing some kind of experiment with a massive tank of water. Elara took an involuntary step back when a giant tentacle reached out of the tank and tried to grab her. All around, anywhere you looked, something interesting was happening.

"Welcome to the Observatory of Oddities," Headmistress Nebulina said, sweeping her arm outward in a dramatic fashion. "This is a little part of the school I've decided to dedicate to the more . . . let's say . . . creative students."

Knot looked unsure, slowly stepping back and forth, trying to take in everything at once. "So we're . . . we're not being punished?"

The headmistress laughed. "Did I say that? Oh, no. You three have caused quite a headache for me.

In return, you are now on my short list. There have been very few students to exhibit such out-of-the-box thinking. History has shown that it is best to keep a close eye on any student sharp and careless enough to create a nuclear reaction within a classroom. And it was here that I set up shop when I was a student."

"Was this where you calculated the Impossible Equation?" Beezle asked. "Proving why the Frils' rapid terraforming machines could never work?"

"It was a time when I—and my friends—explored many aspects of terraforming," the headmistress said with a sad half smile. "Though that is the one everyone seems to remember."

Reaching a small office door at the far end of the warehouse, the headmistress stopped and gave a quick knock. There was a loud crashing noise and a series of muffled curses, but eventually the door opened, revealing a species Elara had never seen.

The headmistress purred softly to the round being that stood before them. He appeared to be a ball-like head with a dozen arms attached. His face was flat and wrinkled, his eyes hidden behind a large pair of goggles, and his upper lip adorned with a long drooping mustache that brushed along the floor as he moved—a process done by balancing on his many hands and shifting his weight in an eerie fashion.

The face parted in a sinister smile almost as wide as the head it was attached to, and a rich voice emerged. "Well, hello there, Headmistress. What do you have for me today, new grist for the mill?"

Headmistress Nebulina chuckled. "Allow me to introduce you to Professor Sunderson," she said to the three students. "Roger, keep a close eye on these three for me. Ideally without them destroying the school in the process."

CHAPTER 010

A week had passed and Elara and her friends had not destroyed the school.

However, they had destroyed two portable containment units, sixteen canisters of compressed oxygen, one solid ton of raw dirt, an overripe banana, a really expensive laser array that they hoped wouldn't come out of their scholarship funds, and a very old poster of a kitten. They were all particularly sad about the kitten, especially Knot, who had named it Tweedles.

But in the name of science, sacrifices had to be made. In this case, the sacrifice was made because the three friends had been given a massive amount of extra work. Under the lesson plan that Nebulina had crafted, they were currently attempting a supposedly simple hydrogen-to-oxygen shift without using any of the standard equipment. And it had not been easy. Not at all. Instead of instantly transforming hydrogen molecules into oxygen, the entire experiment violently exploded.

Fortunately, the explosion was contained within the containment unit—a three-foot-tall cylindrical test chamber made of transparent aluminum. Unfortunately, the straps holding the unit in place were broken, sending the whole system bouncing around the room, ricocheting off the reinforced walls and destroying the kitten poster.

Knot tackled the canister while Elara grabbed an injector. One of the first things they had learned was how to use an acid base to stop a chain reaction. The three girls had found this useful until they discovered the concoction was made from the stomach acids of giant sea creatures. Now they just found it kind of gross.

Gross or not, the solution was handy if you were on the verge of atomic destabilization. Elara slammed the injector into the canister and the device filled with fluid. The light inside rapidly dimmed and the violent shaking started to calm.

"That went poorly!" Beezle said happily.

"I wonder if we would do better with smaller containment devices?" Elara mused as she picked up a bunch of knocked-over equipment. Beakers had fallen over, smashed. Several small plastic orbs—containers for holding living micro-organisms—had hit the ground and scattered across the floor like marbles. In short, the lab was a wreck.

Professor Sunderson arrived on the scene moments later, and was soon poking at the still-shaking canister with a long stick. *"Pff."* He snorted. "I heard you three were supposed to be clever. And what do you have here? Black magic! Alchemy! Even before the headmistress scripted her equation, folks had been studying atomic conversion. And yet no one has managed a breakthrough." The professor gestured at the students with his stick.

"Well . . . yeah," Elara said. "Isn't that why we're here? In this special class? To try and do things no one has ever done?"

"Ridiculous. There are no shortcuts in science." The professor's eyes burned into Elara. "You," he said with great emphasis, "would do well to remember that." A bell rang. "And that's all you get from me today. I'll expect a full report on why the previous attempts at your little alchemy trick failed." And with that, all three students groaned as they slumped out of the observatory building, each wondering how they kept making more work for themselves.

"Elara Adele Vaughn!" a loud and angry voice shouted.

Elara and her friends turned abruptly and found themselves face-to-face with a small group of first-year students. The one who spoke was a ringleader of sorts. Elara recognized her as Suue.

"Excuse me, what?" Elara blurted.

One of the other kids spoke up now. "Your little stunt in Thur'uer's class? The one you were banished from?"

Another kid chimed in. "You ruined the class!"

"What are you talking about?" Elara responded, unable to hide the exasperation in her voice. "We blew up the algae in an atomic explosion. You must have seen the tiny sun? Floating in the middle of the classroom?"

"We liked Professor Thur'uer!" Suue shouted.

Elara shook her head. "Whatever. I don't have time for this."

"Oh, you're gonna make the time, farm girl!" Suue

shouted, grabbing Elara's shoulder.

"Ahem." The voice belonged to Knot, who had picked up Suue by the neck of her shirt. "You will not be attacking my friend. No."

"But she . . ." Suue squirmed. "And you . . ."

Knot leaned in and grinned widely. "I what? Go ahead and accuse me. I'm exactly in the mood for it."

The girl scrunched up her face. Elara had to confess, Suue was brave. Or dumb. Or brave and dumb.

"I challenge you!" Suue yelled. "I challenge you to an after-class duel! Behind the stadium!"

The collected gathering of first-years gasped loudly. All except Knot, who simply shrugged with curiosity. "You mean fancy and with swords?"

"She means a robot duel," Elara whispered back. "Like, battle drones."

"Oh," Knot responded in a wistful tone. "I don't know why I'd bother. I have her in my crushing hand right now." For emphasis, Knot squeezed her hand slightly, and Suue gave an audible squeal.

"No!" Elara said quickly. "Maybe she's mean. But I think crushing her might get you in trouble." Elara glared at the angry group of bullies. "Behind the stadium then," she said, trying to sound brave. "Let's go."

"Oh! But we still have class," Beezle said with a

happy chirp. "And it promises to be a particularly engaging seminar, too!"

"Fine. Behind the stadium then," Elara said, focusing on Suue, trying to recapture her glare. "Later."

Soon they were back at the dorms, trying to distract themselves from the upcoming duel, and the three girls were more exhausted than they ever thought possible.

"How are we supposed to do all this schoolwork?" Knot complained. "I barely have enough time to sleep! If we're not working in the observatory, we're running from class to class! It's impossible!"

"Speaking of impossible," Elara noted, "we're supposed to be on the other side of the campus by now. The bell rings in fifteen minutes."

Knot groaned, and in the end, Elara and Beezle practically had to physically push her out of the dorm room and down the stairs. At least they had gotten to know the Grix well enough to learn that she wasn't actually dangerous when drowsy. Knot just snored and was easily embarrassed by it.

"Have you noticed," Beezle said as they steered the half-asleep Knot across campus, "that despite the careful intent of Sunderson's observatory, we are constantly encouraged to take excessive risk?"

"You mean we blow a lot of stuff up," Elara answered.

Beezle nodded sagely. "I find it curious. But also tiring. Not even the embrace of the OverMind fully restores me."

Elara rolled her eyes. "That thing! Did I mention you're still talking in your sleep! Through that weirdo creepy voice?"

"I believe you have mentioned it thirty-seven times now, yes," Beezle said with a sincere smile.

"Count this as thirty-eight, then," Elara snapped. "It was weird and mysterious at first. Now it's just . . . ugh. The OverMind is chatty and demanding! Last night the OverMind wanted chocolate!"

"No," Beezle admitted. "That one was me. And I was sad when chocolate did not happen."

After a particularly long-winded class lecture on the various minerals that can be extracted from planetary rings, Elara and her friends made their way to the stadium. The STS Stadium was built from an impossibly enormous shell, with rows of seats carved into the curved interior and a large triangular playing field built into the basin.

The group of first-years gathered out back near the storage facilities for robotic drones. These drones served as athletes in most of the school's sports— particularly the galactic favorite, AtomiBall. Heavy, easy to control, and easier to repair, these drones were used on the playing field while students mentally controlled them.

"This should not be happening," Beezle pointed out as Knot slipped on the psionic robot control device.

"We can't back down to bullies," Elara said. "If we do, they'll keep trying to start fights. There was this one boy on the farm when I was a kid, always trying to show off. If I hadn't stood up to him—"

"No," Beezle interrupted. "Though your tale of the farm is certainly fascinating and full of life lessons, my larger point is that there is no cause for a fight. No one was hurt during our incident in class."

"Yeah," Knot replied, jabbing a bulky stone thumb over her shoulder. "Tell them that."

Behind her, Suue was already linked to a robot drone. The robot, a large blocker-bot designed to break other robots, responded to Suue's moves and smashed its fists together.

Elara placed a hand on Beezle's shoulder. "I know. We'll figure it out." In the background, Suue stomped the ground heavily with her feet, and her robot mimicked her movement. The ground under the robot's massive foot cracked just a little bit. "After this."

Knot clicked on the psionic headband, summoning her robot from the stadium's storage shed.

Elara groaned when she saw Knot's selection.

Knot's robot was thin and small. It had two long arms with wide spatula-like hands at the ends and a single glowing green eye.

"A Piercer?" Elara asked, appalled. "You can't fight a Blocker with a Piercer!"

"I do not understand," Beezle said. "We do not play any robot games on my world. What is a Piercer?"

Knot answered, flexing her arm and tentatively testing out her bot. Its thin arm flexed, comically wispy next to the heavy robot Suue was controlling.

"A Piercer is designed to find openings in the opposing team's defense," Elara answered "It's more for evasion and quick movements. Not combat."

The opposing robot stamped its massive feet again. Suue was growing impatient.

Knot glared in response. "Don't worry. I got this."

"Quick movements!" Elara coached. "Keep her off guard. Use your speed to your advantage."

"Come on!" Suue yelled. "Let's get this over with!"

Knot turned, and her robot walked over to Suue's. Ready for a fight, Suue's robot flexed its giant hydraulic muscles and swung a mighty fist in the direction of Knot's robot.

"Dodge!" Elara yelled. "Dodge her!"

Knot cocked her head and simply shrugged. The giant Grix had other plans.

On the field, the tiny Piercer stood its ground. Rather than dodge, Knot's robot took the hit full-on. A spark of electricity shot off its armor.

Suue and her friends howled at the carnage. "That was too easy! What's the matter? Did you forget how to blow things up?"

It didn't look good. Elara watched as Knot's Piercer began to wobble. She put her hand on Knot's rocklike shoulder. "It's okay," she said, accepting defeat.

"Look!" Beezle called out, pointing at the Piercer. The damaged robot swayed, but did not fall.

Elara let out a sigh of relief.

Knot smiled as she commanded her robot to jab up with its spatula-like hands, slicing at the armpit of the larger Blocker.

"Nooooooo!" Suue cried out as the Piercer cut through a weak spot in her bulky robot's armor. The entire limb of Suue's robot fell off.

"You're not allowed to do that," Suue blurted out.

The crowd of students gaped, openmouthed. "I've never seen a move like that," Elara whispered. "Piercers aren't supposed to play aggressively!"

"Why not?" Knot asked, and with another quick swipe, her robot lashed out and severed the other arm on Suue's blocker.

"I no longer have any idea," Elara responded.

"No, you don't!" Suue shouted in anger. Her injured robot was starting to twitch, broken wires and circuit boards overloading its system. Suue kicked her legs and flailed her arms, but her armless robot soon collapsed in a shower of sparks and crumpled metal.

"Noooo!" Suue shrieked, not used to losing.

And just like that, the fight was over. Elara rushed toward Knot and gave her a giant hug, clearly impressed with the Grix's skill. The crowd dispersed, and though she shot a dirty look, even Suue knew when she was beaten.

Elara lay facedown on her bed. Knot was hunched over, reading the history of AtomicBall, which she had declared her new obsession.

"It says here," the Grix explained, "that there have only been seventeen silicon-based players in the major leagues. That seems horribly imbalanced. Silicon life-forms make up sixty-three percent of the galactic population!"

"I'm too tired to process the injustice of that," came Elara's muffled voice.

"Well," Knot added, "there was a briefly lived Silicon league, but that only lasted three seasons before funding was cut. *Tsk*. How horrible."

"That is, indeed, bad. However, I think maybe we should be more concerned with why no one seems to like us," Beezle suggested.

"Maybe they were just looking for an excuse to fight?" Knot added, not looking up from her book.

"No." Beezle shook her head. "I think instead it might have to do with the status of Professor Thur'uer's course on subatomic studies. It appears that it no longer exists."

"What?" Elara asked, sitting up. "So what's Thur'uer teaching?"

"She isn't," Beezle responded, pointing to a class schedule chart on her communicator. "She has left the school altogether. Apparently, quite abruptly, and the class has ended as a result."

Knot scratched her head. "We have a mystery, then."

Just then, all three of the students' wrist

communicators buzzed. Elara checked and saw a message. Reading it, she dropped her head back down, her feeling of exhaustion only climbing. It was proving to be that kind of day.

"We've got to go," she said. "We've been summoned . . . for a field trip."

CHAPTER 011

The small ship rocketed across the horizon.

Inside the school transport, Elara felt as uncomfortable as could be. One: The ship was going very, very fast. Two: This was her first field mission—a trip to the Untamed Valleys on the Southern Hemisphere of Paragon. The Untamed Valleys were designed so that students could attempt some of the more extreme and hazardous terraforming techniques. Because of this, the region was something of an unknown quantity. Older students said that the valleys were different every year, and that even the teachers didn't know what lurked in that zone.

Fortunately, Elara was called up in the same group as her friends. Unfortunately, the mission involved being split into pairs. While Knot and Beezle had been put together, Elara found herself sitting with an unfamiliar boy—a four-armed Suparian named Sabik.

"You've really never been in a class E23 shuttle before?" Sabik asked Elara. The boy was clearly shocked, as if class E23 was something that Elara should have known about.

"Um. No. I grew up on a farming world—Vega Antilles V of Sector 17," she answered. "Not a huge amount of shuttles there."

"But what about when you go to other worlds? I mean, you can't just hop on a T1-12 and call it a day. This shuttle . . ." Sabik rapped the shuttle ceiling with his knuckles and sniffed disdainfully. "It would probably fall apart outside of the hyperspace lane. It's just the bare minimum, really."

Not wanting to pursue the conversation, Elara shifted the topic. "So you like ships, I guess?"

Sabik smiled widely. "Ships. Hyperspace gates. Uncharted warp travel. Everything about it. I'm going to be a pathfinder someday. That's why I'm here. To be the best."

"Ah . . . but the STS Pathfinder program isn't open to first-year students, right?"

"No." Sabik frowned. "It isn't. And even then it's hard to get into. That's why I need to prove myself on this mission. So follow my lead. I'll make sure we get through in record time."

Elara felt her eyes rolling but stopped them in time. She had already been in one fight today. A second wasn't really on her to-do list—especially with someone who was supposed to be her teammate. "Well, we're partners. So how about we just work together, okay?"

Sabik smiled. "How many planets have you even been on?"

"Until coming to school I'd never been off Vega Antilles V. Paragon is my first off-world experience."

"Oh. Oh, that can't even be true," Sabik said, full of disbelief.

Elara decided that she had a right to be irritated now. "I'm not lying. My planet was remote. It's a farm world. Where do you come from, anyway?"

"Suparian Prime—Third World of the Galactic Core. Intergalactic travel is considered a standard part of the education system on all of the capital planets. By age eight, you have to travel to each of the seven worlds and visit the council buildings."

"That's . . . that's just not possible on the outer-rim worlds," Elara answered. "I mean, we learned about other worlds. We had holo-libraries. So it was kind of like being there. But our school was small. We didn't have big shuttle trips to the core worlds. How could we?"

Sabik nodded sympathetically as if he understood. "Huh. I guess in a farming sector, standards are really different. Must make the classes here a challenge."

Elara stared at the Suparian so hard, she was certain it must be burning his flesh. Apparently not, as he failed to burst into flames.

"Excuse me," she said. "Science is science. It doesn't matter where I'm from. The science isn't going to change."

"I dunno. Experience does, though." Sabik gestured at Elara as if everything he was saying should have been obvious. "And how many high-tech labs have you worked in? Did you have an internship or take pre-STS chem classes? Did they even offer those on your world?"

"You know what . . . ?" Elara started to say, an angry tone in her voice. But before she could continue, the intercom activated, and the commander made an announcement.

"Attention, class," came the voice of Commander Bryce, a canine-like flight and survival instructor. "Make sure you're strapped in. We're gonna be landing in a few moments. Remember, though this is our world, that doesn't make this trip risk-free. Far from it. A landing on any planet could be dangerous or even deadly. So say 'hi' to your seatmate. They're going to be your survival buddy for the day. Your life, and theirs, depend on your mutual cooperation and a respect for your partner."

Elara glanced at Sabik, who was now staring disinterestedly out the window. "I'm doomed," she muttered to herself.

The transport ship touched down just on the fringe of the Musstari Desert, an area covered in steep rocky outcroppings. The mission was simple. Each team of two had to race to a series of checkpoints, collecting rock samples along the way. The first team to get back wasn't necessarily the winner. Each sample had to be taken perfectly. Failure to deliver a usable sample was an immediate disqualification—which meant a failing grade.

Elara had managed to squeeze in a visit to the commander's office before launch to ask about the harsh grading. The old soldier had turned to her and laughed.

"You think it's hard now?" he barked, his long wolflike snout showing teeth. "Wait until you're in the field for real. You know what an error means on an inhospitable world?"

Elara started to answer, but the silver-furred canine leaned in close. "It means you're dead! You hear that? You want to die, maybe?" Commander Bryce poked Elara in the forehead for emphasis.

"Yes sir!" Elara stammered. "I mean, no sir. No!"

But Commander Bryce wasn't done with Elara quite yet. "You know the things I've seen? Thirty years of service as a pathfinder in the Affiliated Worlds' terraforming initiative? I've warped over a thousand instances, each one unshielded. The raw energy of creation itself pouring over me."

The commander gripped his fist tight and thumped it across his chest. "I've been dropped on worlds where the oceans are acid, and the only land explodes when you try to walk on it. I've seen dust storms that were sentient, trees that scream like babies, frozen mountains . . . you name it."

Sitting back in his comfortable-looking chair, the commander relaxed. "And you know what I've learned, Ms. Vaughn? I'll tell you . . ."

Commander Bryce looked directly at Elara, his beady eyes boring into her own. A single bead of sweat escaped the young first-year student's forehead, but Elara managed to keep her wits about her. The old commander reached into his desk drawer and pulled out something shiny, handing it to Elara.

"Always carry . . . THIS."

It was a small plastic container of dental floss. Elara looked down at it and then back up at the teacher, who was smiling widely and earnestly. Not knowing what else to do, she took the offering and slowly backed out of the office.

Reflecting back on it now, Elara had to admit that the exchange still made absolutely no sense. But that sort of weird behavior was normal after too many unshielded warp jumps.

"Did you know," Sabik was saying, "that even though there are over three thousand official pathfinders, they only discover an average of three worlds qualified for terraforming per sector? Without worlds to work on, the job opportunities for graduates are going to be slim . . ."

Elara looked up. "That's too bad, I guess. I mean . . . I'm planning on focusing on ecology and bioengineering."

Sabik cut her off, his voice coming out in a hiss. "But without pathfinders, what is there for you to bioengineer? We need new worlds, and only the very best can navigate space without a transwarp tube to guide them!"

"Well, I mean I guess," she conceded. "But there are lots of free traders that do it, too, and sky pirates."

"Bottom-feeders and criminals," Sabik snorted. "My father would have outlawed all unshielded hyperdrive access if the council hadn't been so stubborn!"

"Who's your father?"

Sabik looked surprised, as if the answer should have been obvious. But before he could respond, the students had the wind knocked out of them as the ship slammed to a landing position. Commander Bryce stepped out of the pilot's seat, his metal prosthetic leg gleaming in the light from the shuttle windows.

"Listen up, cadets!" the commander shouted. "Under each seat you will find all the basic gear you need to survive an inhospitable environment. Hold on to your pack tightly, as it could mean the difference between your life and failure."

Each student reached under their seat, finding the small pocket-size emergency kit. Elara opened hers. Inside was a small wrist communicator designed for harsh environments, three signal flares, a flask of condensed water, and a standard nutrition bar. She couldn't help but notice the lack of dental floss and patted her pocket where the spool was tucked away.

"You might think you're just children," the commander continued as the students strapped on the wrist devices. "That this is a school exercise and that you're not at any risk. Well . . . understand this!" he roared. "You are here to learn. You are here to learn to be scientists and designers and trailblazers. And none of that means a thing if you don't know how to survive in space. This will not be easy just because you are children!"

The commander slammed a hatch button with his fist. The door to the transport swung open with more force than any of the students were expecting. Outside, the wind was howling. The air smelled like burning, and waves of heat poured into the small cabin.

"Just outside this transport you will see a color-coded circular marker. Walk through one, and you'll be teleported to the region where your next sample is to be collected. Then your next marker will appear in the distance. These will guide you on the safest route. But don't let that make you lazy! Be prepared to search and struggle! And don't forget, the first team back gets the ultimate reward—respect."

With that, the commander gave a sharp burst on a whistle.

"GO!"

CHAPTER 012

They went. Twelve teams, twenty-four students, all bolted for the door at once. With the obvious exception of Beezle and Knot, most of them were strangers to Elara. She had seen a few of them around, even knew one or two of their names. But she had never spoken to any of them.

Elara was one of the first to reach the door. Once outside, she almost choked. It was hard to believe she was on the same world as the school. All the way around the globe and far south of the equator, it was as close to a different climate as you could get. The ship had landed on a rocky mesa. Surrounding the platform was a large doughnut-shaped valley, filled with roaring winds and heavy amounts of reddish dust below.

"Okay," Elara said to Sabik. "Let's search together and—"

"This way!" Sabik yelled. Suddenly Sabik whirled and began running toward an unseen destination, straight down into the valley. Elara muttered under her breath and followed. The short Suparian proved to be deft on his feet, and Elara was having a hard time keeping up.

And just like that, Sabik was gone, his thin short frame leaping quicker than Elara would have expected off a smooth rock and through the glowing red teleport gate. Elara jumped through after him, materializing halfway down the valley. But she was almost instantly blinded. The swirling sandstorm was too thick, and there was no sign of Sabik.

She tapped her wrist communicator. "Sabik! Where are you! We're a team! We have to work together!" No response.

Elara shook her head. It was one thing to be stubborn and condescending on a shuttle. But in the field, a terraformer had to be all business. That was the point of this training exercise, to succeed as a team.

"Right," Elara said, carefully inspecting the ground for a mineral sample. With no mineral sample, they might as well give up now. And she had a feeling that Sabik had left her behind to do the hard science while he did the exploring.

Thinking she saw a glimpse of another red gate in the distance, Elara carefully slid down the smooth rock and into the heart of the sandstorm. It hit her like a fist, and for a moment she was blind and gagging. Then suddenly, as she slipped down faster into the valley, she felt clean air on her face. The sandstorm was only a thin layer, floating at the upper layer of the valley. Below that layer, the weather was much more tolerable, and Elara could clearly see Sabik standing in the gorge, looking frustrated.

"You didn't answer my call," Elara said grumpily to Sabik. "We're supposed to be a team. You should have waited for me."

"Yes." Sabik nodded quickly. "I should have waited . . ."

"Yes!" Elara yelled, channeling her irritation. "We are a TEAM! That's the mission. If you want to scrub out, fine! But do it on your own time. I worked like crazy to get here, and I'm not going to fail this exercise because you don't think I'm worth working with!"

"Can we just forget all that for a minute?"

"No!" Elara continued. "You don't get to make me mad, then decide I shouldn't be mad! What is wrong with you?"

Sabik's eyes were wide as he responded, "It's my leg."

Elara was confused. "Your leg? Wait. What's wrong with your leg?"

Sabik was pale. "There's something wrapped around it."

Elara looked down and saw a slimy green tentacle wrapped around the Suparian's leg. It was thin with purple suction cups, and it seemed to have a very tight grip.

"Oh," Elara said, completely caught off guard. "Yeah. We should probably talk about my thing later."

Suddenly the tentacle yanked on Sabik, and the small Suparian was dragged toward the cliff wall.

"SABIK!" Elara yelled.

"GAHHHH!" Sabik responded.

And then he was gone, pulled into a small cavern in the cliff wall that Elara hadn't noticed before.

Elara wasted no time, covering the distance in seconds. Reaching the dark cave opening, she tapped on the wrist device twice in rapid succession to activate the flashlight beam. The cavern was dry, and the floor was covered in sand. *That was useful*, Elara thought, as she could see which way the tentacle had grabbed Sabik. Shining her light left and right, she was surprised to see how vast the cavern was. It stretched for at least forty feet on either side, with multiple passageways in the distance. And, as if the problem wasn't bad enough, Sabik's wrist communicator was on the ground, lost during his tussle with the giant tentacle.

Elara grabbed it and tucked it in her satchel. The monster's trail led across and to the left of the cavern, disappearing into another passageway. Elara ran to it, shouting Sabik's name as she did. That was a mistake. More tentacles emerged—at least two or three from every cave opening. The tentacles slithered across the ground toward her faster than Elara thought possible. With a quick jump, she dodged one, only to have another tangle in her arm. With a quick twist, she wrenched herself free and dived into the cavern opening that Sabik had been dragged into.

Elara landed on her face, striking her head hard on a jagged rock. She whirled and was almost certain that tentacles would grab her. But before they could, she felt herself slip. *That was the problem with diving headfirst into a dark cave*, Elara thought. You never knew exactly what you'll find.

In this case, she found a very steep and slippery slope.

Elara tumbled and slipped and rolled down the slope, bouncing off rocks as she went. Finally, with a thud, she managed to crash into a sand-covered cave floor. *Well*, she thought. *Not just sand. Something else, too. Something crunchy . . .*

Tapping at her wrist light to reactivate, she saw what she had fallen on. Bones. Lots and lots of bones. From animals of some kind.

Bones on their own didn't bother Elara. She grew up on a farm. She had seen worse. But this pile . . . Elara gulped. It wasn't like this was a graveyard.

It was a den. And these bones were the remains of meals.

Elara set the creepiness aside for a moment. Her teammate came first.

"Sabik! Where are you?"

There was a pause. Then she heard Sabik yell a response.

"In . . . a cave?"

"That's not helping!" she called back.

"Well, it's not like I could take down the address!" the distant voice of Sabik shouted back.

"Okay," Elara muttered to herself. "The yelling was coming from the left. I'm pretty sure it was from the left. I hope."

Reaching into her pocket, Elara pulled out the spool of dental floss and quickly tied the end of the thread to a rocky outcropping, issuing a silent thanks to the commander as she did so. At the very least, she'd be able to find her way back. And with that, Elara stepped into the maze of passageways, running left, right, right, left toward the sound of Sabik's voice. The search took some time, and Elara had to double back more than once. She was about to give up and return to the shuttle for help when she noticed a small passage leading into the ceiling. It was difficult, but she managed to climb into it. The tunnel swerved and twisted and dropped back down again a dozen feet, finally ending in a massive cave. The cavern was covered in a glowing moss of some kind, so Elara dimmed her flashlight and crept forward, looking for a sign of Sabik.

He was below, caught in some kind of large web. It was almost a horrific sight, but the glowing moss and glittering web created a strangely beautiful rainbow effect. What was less beautiful was the creature that had spun the web. Sabik couldn't see it, his eyes were covered in webbing, but Elara got a look at the beast. It was a giant spider of some sort. Well, it had the body of a spider, anyway. Where its eight legs should have been was a mass of tentacles. Where one would expect a face there was a massive orange beak with two eye-stalks that wobbled with such ferocity it was almost comical. But as the creature opened its massive beak, and its forked tongued rolled out, Elara decided comical was probably the last thing the creature was. It was a monster, and it had her classmate captive, and there was nothing funny about it.

Then the creature roared. Sort of. It kind of squeaked. Then it purred. It sounded so much like an angry kitten that it was almost impossible for Elara to look away.

"Elara?" Sabik called out. "Anytime would be good. I think the tentacles that grabbed me might be getting hungry."

Elara quickly searched her survival kit. Grabbing a flare and ripping the pin, she jumped from her hiding place and skidded down a rocky slope toward the den of the creature. The thing whirled, startled by the sudden noise.

"Hey, monster! Check this out!"

The flare was sparking, and Elara hurled it over the creature's head. The spider's eye-stalks tracked the light, and the giant monster turned and bounded after the distraction. Elara climbed up the web, careful to avoid any particularly sticky strand, and grabbed at Sabik to pull him free.

"Is that you?" Sabik shouted. "Get this stuff off my eyes!"

Elara ripped the web strand from Sabik's eyes, which unfortunately took a thin layer of his skin with it.

"AGH! WHY?" Sabik yelped in shock from the pain.

"Quiet!" Elara whispered as she hacked at the strands with a jagged rock she had found.

"We don't have much time!"

"Well, maybe you shouldn't have taken so long to find me!"

"I didn't have to look for you at all!"

"Yes, you did! We're partners! You said we have to work together!"

Elara considered slapping a sticky piece of webbing over Sabik's mouth but opted instead to cut the Suparian loose. Unfortunately, they were both fifteen feet in the air, and the cranky alien boy dropped to the ground, slamming hard into the rocky floor.

"GLUK!" Sabik said.

"Oops," Elara responded.

She dropped down and pulled Sabik up to his feet.

"I guess I should thank you," Sabik grumbled.

"You could," Elara said, looking past Sabik and down the depths of the caverns. The spider creature had grown bored with the flare and was now slowly slithering toward them.

"Or actually, maybe instead we should just run. Let's run, okay?"

Sabik, who hadn't actually seen the thing, looked over his shoulder and grew horribly pale.

"That is so much worse than it sounded," he whispered. "It sounded like a kitten."

Elara whispered back, "This would be so much better if it *was* a giant kitten."

"Prrr!" purred the horrific spider-monster sweetly. And then it leapt.

"Left!" Elara shouted. "Turn left!"

The two classmates ran at breakneck speed down the corridors, following Elara's trail of dental floss. The strategy was working, but they could feel the monster's hot breath on the back of their necks.

"We're trapped!" Sabik shrieked when he saw that the dental floss trail led twenty feet straight up.

"This way!" Elara yelled, grabbing Sabik by one of his four arms and dragging him down a side passage.

Suddenly Elara felt a buzzing in her pocket—her communicator! She had checked it a dozen times since this started but hadn't been able to get a signal. The commander must have noticed they were overdue and was checking in.

Elara fumbled to wrestle her comm from her pocket and quickly answered. "Commander Bryce? Is that—"

The voice on the other end came through crackly and barely audible. But it definitely wasn't the commander. "Danny?" Elara asked. "Is that you?" Looking at her comm, she realized that this might be the only chance she got. "Sorry! Gotta go! Call you later!"

Sabik grabbed Elara's arm and yanked her to the left. While running, Elara tried to ping the commander. No reception. Of course.

Behind the two students was a cacophony of shrieking.

"It's right behind us!" Sabik yelled.

"I can see that!" Elara yelled back. "Keep running!"

The pair dodged and ducked and weaved. The caverns in the cliff side were endless. Even if they escaped the monster . . . how long would they last? How long could they last? There was no sign of a way out. But the shrieking continued, and all they could do was run. And then they reached a sheer drop, a gorge inside a cavern.

"Whoever the geologist was that thought up these designs . . . I want to have a word with them," Sabik muttered.

"Wait a minute . . . ," Elara said with a snap of her fingers.

Sabik turned. "It's getting closer . . ."

"No! Think!" Elara said as she scrambled in the dirt.

"We're still on our mission. We have to gather mineral samples!"

"Are you freaking kidding me?!" Sabik screamed. "We're about to be eaten!"

"If we get our next sample, we'll activate the teleport ring! It's an automated system! It doesn't matter where we are!"

Suddenly Sabik dropped to his knees and started digging next to Elara. "What are we looking for?"

"Our second sample . . . some kind of crystallite mineral. Something with refraction capabilities. Caused through internal tectonic pressure . . ."

"Here!" Sabik yelled, holding up a small fragment of crystal. It was tiny, but it seemed to fit the bill. "Scan it!" the Suparian yelled. "SCAN IT!"

The spider-kitten monster was wagging its wide behind now. It was ready to let loose a life-ending pounce.

"I scanned it!" Elara yelled. "It's scanned!"

"Is that . . . ," Sabik said, "is that a red ring?"

Elara whipped her head around, staring deep into the shadows. Far below, she could see it. A leap of faith.

"It is. It's the next marker. It's our path."

"But . . . how?" Sabik said, shaking his head in disbelief. The kitten-monster purred loudly. It coiled its legs and sprang.

"It's supposed to guide us to the safest path!" Elara said, remembering the commander's words. "So jump!"

Elara grabbed Sabik's hand and jumped off the edge of the gorge toward the ring. Propelling through the darkness with the monster's screams around them, the pair fell through the red ring. With a quick, shimmering sensation, they teleported once more, materializing near the shuttle, several feet above the ground. With a sudden shout, they dropped, landing with a thud and finally skidding to a stop at the prosthetic foot of a grumpy and impatient-looking Commander Bryce.

"Took you long enough," he said sternly.

CHAPTER 013

Σ lara found herself back in the office of the headmistress—this time without her friends. Sabik was with her, so that was . . . something? They were both tired and dirty and covered in spider-kitten webs. But apparently, almost getting eaten by a dangerous mutated monster was something that teachers wanted to talk about immediately.

"And so I followed Sabik in," Elara explained for what felt like the zillionth time, "and I was attacked by a bunch of tentacles, and I dived into a cave . . ."

"Meanwhile I was tied up to a big web. And she saved me. And then we escaped," Sabik said with a glare. "Can we go now? My feet hurt."

"Bah!" Commander Bryce barked. "You've both been thoroughly scanned, and you sustained zero substantial injuries."

Headmistress Nebulina held up a furry paw. "Commander . . . please. These children have been through an ordeal, even if they are not physically injured."

"Well, they shouldn't have been playing in the caves! In fact, they shouldn't have even been in that quadrant!" The dog-faced commander leaned in. "What were you doing down there, anyway? The truth this time!"

"We've told you the truth!" Elara yelled back. "Your stupid teleport thing sent us right in front of the cave! Whose fault is that?!"

The headmistress tapped her desk with one long fingernail. "A fair question. One we will certainly be investigating. What's important is that you are both back on school grounds, unhurt. And if I'm not mistaken, successful in your class project, too?"

"Now, that's just ridiculous!" the commander grumbled.

Elara pulled off her mission wrist device. "This has

all the stuff on it we scanned. All the samples. We found everything, or the teleport wouldn't have brought us back, right?"

"But it's hardly the point! You went off mission parameters. You didn't follow protocol! There should be a full investigation! A hearing!"

"Time and place, Commander," Nebulina purred, focusing her eyes on Elara. "What we know right now is that our young Ms. Elara—and her friend—are both much more capable than your average first-year student. Good thing, too."

The headmistress stood up. "Now, why don't the two of you return to your dorms and get some rest. If there are any more questions, I will send for you. But otherwise," she said with a pointed glance at the commander, "I think it best if we just put this mishap behind us. Yes?"

The commander grumbled and made his way out the door. Elara and Sabik got up from their chairs to leave as well, but the headmistress put a soft hand on Elara's arm and stopped her.

"Elara, a quick word if you don't mind."

Sabik gave Elara a curious glance but headed for the main door. The headmistress sat quietly for a moment, as if contemplating something. Finally, as Elara began to squirm, she spoke.

"I've been taking a look at your file, Elara. And I must say, your résumé is very impressive."

"Résumé?" Elara responded, shrugging. "You mean, like, the stuff I've done? We're only a few weeks into the semester."

"I'm looking more at your endeavors before coming to this school. You know admission into the STS is very limited. We only accept one out of every ten thousand applicants. We have to be selective. The school is in high demand, and there is only so much room, after all."

The headmistress glanced at some papers at her desk. "But your test scores were impressive. Your application thesis was certainly compelling. 'The Cost of Progress—an Examination of Extinct Species.' Very interesting. And apparently, by age eight you had repaired a critical weather station in your hometown."

Elara shuffled her feet. "It wasn't that big of a deal. It was just some busted-up signal boosters."

"Don't undervalue what you did. There are far too many in this galaxy that will do that for you. No . . . it says here that your intervention came just in time to stop a potential flood. You saved lives. At the age of eight. Very impressive."

"Um . . . thanks?"

The headmistress leaned in close.

"It also says here that you have a history of getting into trouble. Like reprogramming the harvest machines to make patterns in the fields, and trying to stow away on a low-orbit satellite?"

Elara's eyes shifted off to one side. "That first one . . . it really was an accident."

"Well," Headmistress Nebulina said with a smile, "accidents will happen. And I have no doubt that you will be very careful now that you are here with us at the Seven Systems School of Terraforming Sciences and Arts. You have a very bright future ahead of you. Very bright, I can see that. But it is up to you to make sure you make the most of the chances you are given. In the observatory and otherwise."

The headmistress stood up. "Again, don't worry. You're not in any trouble. Not right now. I've given you a rare opportunity to use your gifts. And I've looked at the reports you've written for Sunderson. But I really need to see more from you. I think you need a little more direction. So I thought maybe you might try solving . . . this."

The headmistress pushed a file folder across the desk to Elara. Hesitantly, as if the papers inside might bite, the young girl opened the folder. She read the opening paragraph of the thesis inside: *The Impossible Equation*, as calculated by Kyrsten Nebulina.

"This . . ." Elara went pale. "I can't do this. It's . . . impossible. You know that."

"Of course," Nebulina answered patiently. "I don't expect you to actually solve it. I expect you to try."

"You want me to try and do something I can't do?"

"Yes. Absolutely," Nebulina answered. Walking across the office, she stopped at the massive bronze plaque that hung on her wall. The equation was all there, emblazoned in metal for all to see. "Gifted to me a few years ago when I assumed my current position," she explained. "You have to understand," she said as she ran one finger down the surface of the plaque, "this equation is the very foundation of our work. Proof that terraforming takes time and patience. It cannot be done instantaneously. But if we do not *try* to do the impossible . . . we can never really know our true potential."

She turned back to Elara. "So show me you believe in yourself enough to try. Show me what you can do. Have your friends help you, too—including that boy, Sabik. Whatever you need to make this work . . . make it work."

And with that, Elara left the office.

Sabik was waiting for her outside the door. "What did she say?" he asked. "Any thoughts on the teleporter thing? Or what they're going to do about the spider-monster?"

Elara shook her head. "No. Just . . . she gave me a special assignment."

"Oh," Sabik said, clearly disappointed. "That's not very interesting at all. I mean, I want to know why I was almost eaten!"

"All right." Elara glanced at her comm system. "Knot and Beezle should be at the observatory. You'd better come meet my other friends. Better if I only have to explain this once."

"Other friends," Sabik said with a raised eyebrow. "Does that mean we're friends now?"

"I should have left you in that cave," Elara observed.

"This . . . this is ridiculous," protested Sabik. "How is it you three have had access to these facilities? This wasn't listed in the curriculum guide!"

Beezle and Knot had been hesitant to let Sabik into their circle but were curious to hear how the pair had escaped certain death. Elara expected more pushback, but everyone was overworked, and a distraction was welcome.

"It's a special projects lab for . . . for special students," Elara said. "You have to be invited."

"Well, I wasn't invited! I'm special!"

"To clarify," Beezle interjected, "the designation

'special' in this instance refers to careless students considered at high risk for blowing things up."

"Oh," Sabik responded, mollified. "Okay, that's fair. That sounds a lot like Elara."

"Yes." Beezle nodded with an innocent smile. "She has blown up many things these last few weeks! She has proven quite talented at destruction!"

"Not helping, Beezle," Elara responded.

Knot sat down heavily on a chair. "Why is he here again?"

"The headmistress has some thoughts on what we should be studying." And with that, Elara pulled out the folder with the Impossible Equation and explained exactly what was expected of them all.

"I changed my mind," Sabik muttered after a long silence. "I don't want to be invited."

"Where would we even start?" Knot asked. "I mean, the Impossible Equation isn't possible. That's the whole point. Rapid terraforming is a disaster! So . . ."

Elara sighed. "That's what I told the headmistress. But she wants us to try."

Beezle picked up the folder of papers and stared at it intently. After a moment, she gasped and held her hand to her mouth in an expression of surprise. Everyone practically jumped out of their chairs.

"What?" Elara asked hurriedly. "What is it?

Did you figure something out?"

Beezle shook her head with a sad smile. "No. I wondered if I might trick myself into suddenly realizing the answer, as if it had been obvious the entire time. Much like conclusions are often drawn during dramatic points in holo-fictions."

Sabik glared heavily. "Well, this isn't a holo-fiction. It's a very insane piece of homework. And we have to try something!"

Elara took the folder from Beezle and started handing documents out to her friends. "Let's just start with the math. We'll work out where to go once we've all gotten a good look at it and—" Elara stopped and held up a hand. "Wait . . . ," she said. "Do you hear that?"

Everyone did. It was two adults, yelling at each other.

Elara quickly pushed her friends behind a nearby bookcase.

"Why are we hiding?" Sabik hissed quietly.

"I just don't want to deal with any more angry teachers today. Unless you want more homework?" Elara answered.

"Quiet!" growled Knot, pushing herself between the two of them.

Peering between books, Elara could see Professor Sunderson. He was agitated and arguing with another figure. But who he was arguing with was just out of sight, and their voices barely carried.

". . . quantum energy!" said the unseen person.

". . . explain . . . stunt?" Sunderson fired back. "You know . . . Groob . . ."

"Explain everything . . . future . . . imperfect. Follow—" the stranger said. And then the shadowy figure turned and stormed away. In the distance, Elara heard a door slam.

The stranger—a tall, thin man Elara didn't recognize—walked past the bookshelf. Elara felt the sudden urge to sneeze but managed—barely—to suppress it. They were all as silent as a grave. Still, the man paused for a moment, his head tilting.

He approached the bookshelf, stopping just on the other side of the students. Elara felt her knees shake. Maybe it had been a bad idea to hide. They had every reason and right to be in the observatory. But something about the argument they had overheard had put Elara on edge, and it was impossible to say how the stranger or Sunderson would react to having been eavesdropped on.

The stranger reached up with one hand, practically right to Elara's face. She pulled back deeper into the shadows in the hopes that he hadn't actually seen any of them.

And yet . . . all he did was pull out a book. He tucked it under his arm and continued walking toward the small office Sunderson kept in an upstairs corner of the warehouse. It was a very thick and weathered-looking hardcover. Elara leaned slightly so she could catch a glimpse of the cover as the stranger walked toward Sunderson's office.

The title was *The Empire That Did Not Care*.

Elara whispered those words to herself, hearing them once more in the voice of the OverMind, remembering that first night with Beezle, and she felt her skin grow even colder.

CHAPTER 014

It had been three weeks since Elara and Sabik had escaped their doom at the hands of the spider-kitten, and things had seemed to settle down. There was no news about the field-trip disaster, no messages from the OverMind, and no clue as to what was in that mysterious book. Elara's friends were too tired to pursue the problems, and Elara herself was beginning to wonder if she was paranoid. To further distract matters, Visitors Day was on the horizon, and most students were focused on their end-of-semester tests and setting up plans to meet with their friends or families. Danny had messaged several times, but Elara was having trouble concentrating on anything that normal.

Instead, she had tried on several occasions to search Sunderson's office to see the book the stranger had taken off the shelf. But it was no use. Sunderson must have taken the book to his own private quarters, and Elara could think of no way to break in there without getting caught.

She had also tried looking the book up, but there was no relevant information on the title recorded. It was a weird mystery. The Galactic Libraries had every book ever written. The absence of this one left Elara even more confused.

But why? And what for? Nothing she could think of made any sense.

Then came the first official STS AtomiBall game of the school year.

Elara and Beezle were sitting with Sabik—who, despite being fairly irritating, had proven to be interesting company. It was Knot's athletic debut. The giant stone Grix girl had fallen in love with the sport after the fight with Suue Damo'n. To her own surprise, she made the team on her first tryout—one of the only first-years to get picked. It really shouldn't have been that shocking. It turned out that the coach—a massively built, bright orange Crimioghast named Ares Degovi—had the stadium ground monitored. Having witnessed Knot's obvious skill, the coach had made a space for the Grix available.

The assembled students yelled and cheered as the lights in the arena dimmed and the teams marched out. The seating was split into three groups, one section for fans of each team: the Protons, the Electrons, and the Neutrons.

And then out marched the teams. Elara was ecstatic to see her friend out on the field, even though the players didn't directly play. But still, they were expected to be athletic, and so the preshow drills started up.

"I've never seen this kind of 'game,'" Beezle said, her eyes wide with shock. "I assumed this would be some kind of academic contest. I mean, that is why we are enrolled, so that we can indulge in academic delights, is it not?"

Sabik looked at her like she was crazy. "You don't have the AtomiCorps on your home world? I thought every populated system was part of the ACL." The Suparian was wearing a cap emblazoned with the logo of the Golden Quarks, Galactic champions of the AtomiCorps League and current holders of the Quantum Cup.

"My people generally prefer isolation," Beezle admitted uncomfortably. "There are very few of us willing to distance ourselves from the greatness of the OverMind. And this activity, I believe, runs counter to Arctuiaan philosophies."

Sabik just stared. "But you've never even heard of it? I mean, this is low-level school stuff, but the Galactic-level tournaments are legendary!"

"But why would you want to make robots destroy each other? It seems terribly wasteful."

Elara glanced up and scanned the field. The teams were preparing to go into the immersion chambers so they could begin the first session. "It's a game, Beezle. And the robot drones are all repairable. No harm done."

"So it's okay to break things if they can be fixed? That is not the case on my home world. We consider all things sacred, especially technology. It is to be revered," Beezle said.

"Your home world sounds very dull," Sabik said gravely.

"Sabik!" Elara snapped. "That's rude!"

Elara turned to Beezle. "Look . . . ," she said. "AtomiCorps brings communities together. We unite behind our teams. Their wins and losses become ours. Sports . . . they make us stronger. Not just physically, but culturally."

Sabik shook his head. "No. No, that's not it at all!"

"What?" Elara glared.

"Sure," Sabik said. "If you live on a farming planet and you spend all day in the dirt, you need an escape. But let's be honest, AtomicCorps exists because of money. After terraforming, the ACL is the biggest revenue generator in the galaxy."

Elara rolled her eyes mockingly. "Oh, right. I almost forgot that you're awful. Your father probably owned a team, right?"

"Three, actually. The Salaman Imperium is the largest private sponsor of the ACL. It's deductible, so . . ."

"Shh!" Beezle said. "The display of social violence is about to begin!"

The arena darkened, and then after a dramatic pause, red, blue, and green floodlights illuminated the field. The crowd went wild. The three teams of remote-controlled robots took the corners of the triangular field. A floating black-and-white-striped round robot zoomed around the center of the field, carrying the orange ball of energy. With a quick spin, it blew a whistle and launched the ball into the air.

At the same moment, Interceptors—fast robots with four arms for catching and passing—dashed across the field from each corner, while the Blockers on each team formed a shield wall around their goals. The last set of robots—the Piercers—galloped across the field in a wide arc, ready to strike at any moment.

A Neutron Runner was the first to reach the ball, but only by a half second. The robot turned to bolt toward the Proton goal, but as soon as it stepped across the boundary line, it was smashed almost in half by a Proton Blocker. The orange ball bounced out of the Interceptor's hand and shot across the field, where it was snatched by a Proton Piercer, who turned and bolted toward the Electrons' corner.

The crowd was roaring now. "That's a terrible play!" Sabik sneered. "The Electron defense is locked in. There's no way through!"

Elara had to agree. The Proton Piercer zigged and zagged, but there was no clear path past the wall of Electron Blockers. Not that it mattered. By the rules of the game, the Piercer wasn't allowed to hold on to the ball for more than thirty seconds, and after a moment too long, the robot's body shuddered and collapsed.

The result was a moment of chaos.

"Wait a minute . . . ," Sabik said. "That happened way too fast. The Piercer . . ."

Before he could finish that sentence, the deactivated Piercer bolted upright and struck, using its wide flat hands to trip the approaching Blocker while swatting the ball through the gap in the Electron shield wall.

The crowd went wild as the ball struck the goal and the Proton Piercer scored the first point of the game in a completely unexpected move.

"Oh!" Beezle said. "The robot was only pretending it had deactivated. I did not expect such deceit!"

Elara zoomed in with a pair of binoculars, checking the number painted on the Piercer who scored the point. "Number 33 . . . that's Knot! Her first game and she scored the first point!"

"But it was kind of a cheat, wasn't it? I mean—OW!" Sabik rubbed his arm where the smiling Beezle had struck him.

"You mean you are impressed with your friend's amazing achievement, yes?" Beezle asked with a raised brow.

"Fine. Yes. Wow," Sabik answered through gritted teeth as he rubbed his sore shoulder. "That's . . . It just has to be against regulations . . . ," Sabik said.

After a brief moment of on-the-field debate, the referees decided differently, and the Protons gained a solid point.

The next several plays were the usual destructive fare. There were three robots destroyed by explosions, two that fell into the shifting spiked pits, and one that caught fire.

An hour later and the game was nearing its end. Knot's Piercer was one of the only Proton bots still in play and was paddling the ball back and forth between its wide hands.

And the last seconds of the clock were ticking down.

"GO, KNOT!" Elara yelled.

Two Blockers tried to tackle Knot's nimble Piercer, but the robot moved too fast, ducking and weaving.

But the odds were against the Grix. Blocker after Blocker came after the Piercer, and eventually she was taken down just as the countdown ended. Elara, along with many other students, jumped up and started cheering. The score was 4–3–3, with the Protons in the lead.

"Oh," Beezle said, her face almost sad. "Knot was defeated. Are you celebrating that her robot was destroyed?"

Elara shook her head. "No! I mean, yeah she was tackled, but she kept the ball from the other teams during the last seconds of the game! Points are double during the last minute, so if they would have scored . . ."

"Oh. She sacrificed herself. How sad."

"No . . . it's a win! It's . . . Look, never mind. Just jump up and cheer, okay?"

Beezle dutifully jumped up and began happily

cheering. "Hooray, for senseless destruction! Congratulations on every robot breaking!"

Close enough, Elara decided.

After the game, Sabik headed off to the library, still apparently unhappy with the extremely unorthodox play. Elara and Beezle congratulated Knot. They found their mountainous friend in the black-and-yellow isolation chamber at the base of the bleachers, depowering her drone command unit. She was surrounded by her teammates, most of whom were third-year or higher. It was unusual to make the team as a first-year, but Knot was an unusual student.

"Did you see?!" Knot bellowed when she caught a glimpse of her friends. "They're going to have to rewrite the rule book after that play!"

Beezle gave her best beaming smile. "It was successfully barbaric. You really destroyed those helpless robots with supreme effectiveness."

Knot looked at Beezle sympathetically. "Oh. My poor dear. They don't have sports on your world, do they?"

"Not at all!" Beezle responded, her earnest smile growing even wider.

"It was pretty amazing," Elara said. "I used to watch

all the league games. And even on the pro level, I've never seen that kind of move."

"Yeah, well, to be fair," one of the other players broke in with a laugh, "pro-defense knows better than to lock all its bruisers together in a static wall formation. Smart players keep moving, you know?"

"ACTIVATE. ACTIVATE," a crackly voice interrupted.

"Who said that?" Elara asked, jumping up to look around.

Beezle staggered. "I feel . . . that voice. I can hear it in my head."

"Oh," Knot said, staring out of the booth and onto the field. "Oh. I don't think this is supposed to happen."

Elara pushed her way past several of the players, all of whom were trying to see what was happening. "Omigosh!" Elara whispered. "The robots. They're all . . . they're active? How?"

Elara glanced around. No one had an answer. But there it was. The robots, many of which were broken or disabled, were all moving. Some badly staggering, others just hardly able to crawl. But still they were moving, and moving toward the booth.

Beezle's eyes rolled, and she slumped to the ground. The heavy voice of the OverMind came from her mouth again. "BEWARE, ELARA, BEWARE. THE

EMPIRE THAT DID NOT CARE."

One of the Proton players ripped open a large computer panel. "But the control switch is turned off!" Another player checked an unlocked cabinet filled with circular robot control modules. "The controls are all here. So how . . . ?"

A robot crashed through the reinforced glass window, and suddenly everything was chaos. Players scattered in all directions. Beezle was clutching at the sides of her head in some kind of psychic pain, and Elara found herself backing farther and farther away from an onslaught of robots.

Beezle's voice rose into a fevered pitch as her body started thrashing back and forth. "THEY WERE LOST. LOST, AND THEIR SPIRITS DO ROAM. IN SEARCH OF A NEW, ETERNAL HOME! GROOB IS WATCHING, GROOB IS LISTENING!"

Knot grabbed a bot in her massive stone hand and bellowed a roar Elara had never heard. The robot crumpled in her grasp, and the Grix hurled it back out the window. But instantly two more appeared to take its place.

Elara grabbed Beezle and started dragging the semiconscious Arctuiaan to the door. Almost instantly it was blocked. She looked over her shoulder and saw the robots trying to push past Knot to reach her.

"Eeee . . . llaarr . . . aaa ," groaned one robot through its half-demolished vocalizer.

"AAAHHHGH!" yelled Beezle.

"Knot!" Elara yelled. But the powerful Grix was swarmed with robots. With no other options, she shielded Beezle with her own body and waited for the attack to come. Instead, a piercing shrieking filled the air. The room flickered to darkness for a moment, and then the backup battery lights kicked on. The master power, Elara realized. No matter what had started the robots or who was controlling them, there had to be some kind of power source.

The robots slid off Knot, suddenly inactive. With a grunt, Knot crumpled a robot head in her hands, reducing the metal cranium to an unrecognizable pile of scrap. Beezle was on the ground wheezing while Knot looked around, as if ready to attack, and Elara leaned against the wall, letting out a deep breath she hadn't realized she had been holding.

"What happened?" Knot finally managed.

"They just stopped. It's like . . . whatever was powering them was shut off."

"They were very loud. Loud in my head," Beezle complained, shivering as if cold.

"Um," a voice cut in. It was Sabik, and he was holding a fancy pink box in one hand and an unplugged power cord in the other. "I came back. I decided Knot deserved some cake." The Suparian scanned the room, taking in the wreckage. "To celebrate," he said.

"Yay?" he added, with a shrug.

CHAPTER 015

"Shh!" Elara hissed.

The four friends were sneaking their way through the school's administrative building. Well, technically they were five, as Beezle had insisted on picking up some odds and ends from the observatory, and swinging by the dorm to grab Clare, who was now strapped to Knot's back. It was late, and the entire planet was on sleep cycle—minus a few fairly easy-to-evade security drones.

"We should have waited and talked to someone about the robot attack," Knot complained. "At least I should have told Coach Degovi."

Elara waved the idea away. "Should we? I mean, who do we trust? Besides, they'll know all the basics. The robots attacked. Right now, we barely know more than they did. No . . . ," she continued. "Someone was in control of those. And that someone has access to high-tech school equipment, meaning a teacher. And the robots were specifically after me."

"Maybe . . . ," Sabik grumbled.

"It said my name! They pushed past you, ignored all the other players, and came for me. And one said my name," Elara snapped. "First the teleport gates on our field trip, now this? Don't you think that's too weird to be a coincidence? And the OverMind and the book title? Something strange is going on!"

Sabik was silent for a minute. Then he whispered back, "I guess? Maybe? But even then . . . what can we do?"

"We find out everything we can about the teachers, and figure out which one of them is guilty," Elara suggested.

"Friends," Beezle interrupted. "I know this is difficult. But we must be hasty and make our way into the data vaults. The control system will stay off-line for only seventeen more minutes, and after that, our presence will automatically be detected and recorded into the system's log file."

Getting around the school's security system had been the most difficult part of the expedition. All activity in administrative buildings was monitored and recorded for the sake of safety. Beezle had come up with a two-pronged solution. First, they would reconfigure their comm systems and leave them in the dorm room. Second, they had to move during a routine power reset—just twenty minutes long one night a week. Luckily, this was the night.

Taking one last look around to make sure they were alone, Elara tapped her school communicator, activating the built-in flashlight. The offices were very utilitarian compared to most of the school. High-density white plastic covered almost every surface. A large tinted window overlooked the campus. Most importantly, the building was empty. More than once Elara thought she and her friends were being followed, but every time she turned, there was no one to be seen.

The group reached the far wall. "Through here," Beezle said, gesturing toward a door marked "Archives."

"That looks like the kind of place where we get in the absolute worst trouble if we're caught," Sabik said. "This is a terrible idea?"

127

Knot grimaced as well. "Agreed. But we're doing it, anyway."

"Maybe this is a bad idea," Elara said, thinking about the repercussions for her friends if they were caught. "I mean, maybe I'm wrong. Maybe this is nothing."

Beezle wiggled the door, testing the lock. "I do not believe it is nothing. I believe it is something. Something not good." She looked up at Elara. "You have been reached by the OverMind directly. Once was unusual but could potentially be dismissed. Twice is not a natural event."

"Here," Knot said, gently pushing Beezle out of the way. "I have a knack for picking locks . . ." With that, she flicked a finger, and the door nearly came off the hinges. "See?"

"Wow," said Sabik sarcastically. "Super stealthy."

"Quiet!" Elara hushed, turning to look over her shoulder. Still no one there, but it was better to be safe than sorry. She quickly pushed them through the now-open door. "Why the archives, Beezle?" she said, closing the remains of the door behind them.

Beezle sat down and was rooting around her backpack—something else she picked up when they stopped for Clare. "Ah," she said, smiling. "Here we go. We are very lucky I had thought to bring this item from my home world."

Beezle held up a thin, foldable metallic helmet. It was an odd-looking piece of hardware, with many small lights embedded into its golden surface. It had a sleek and dark visor, and two conduits running from either side. At the end of one conduit was a thin clamp, and at the end of the other was a power jack.

"So this is a what now?" Elara started.

Sabik interrupted. "It's a psionic enhancement helmet. It's like . . . a toy. Unless you already have some kind of psychic abilities."

Knot was confused. "What does it do?"

Sabik gestured at the machine in Beezle's hands as the Arctuiaan attached the clamp to her finger. "You can use it to interface low-level computers. Check messages. Read reports. That sort of thing. It's kind of like the VR helmets you use to control the robots, but it's not tied to any one system."

"Yes," agreed Beezle, lowering the helmet onto her head. "I brought this from home so I could occasionally use it to secure a more direct connection within the OverMind with my family. But with minor modification, I can use this as a signal boost, and if there is a voice trying to reach Elara, we should be able to trace it."

Sabik shook his head. "The helmet's not strong enough. You'd need an external power source.

Something that gave off more energy than any battery."

"Not to worry, friends," Beezle said, pulling the end of the power cable apart and stripping the wires bare. "I believe I have a solution to that particular problem. Meanwhile, Knot, would you please attach these cables to Clare?"

Knot followed Beezle's instructions. Elara glanced at Beezle. "What kind of power source? Beezle? Did you . . . ?"

Beezle opened her bag again, and a bright light poured out. Elara, Sabik, and Knot all flinched away, while the slim Arctuiaan reached in and pulled out a transparent canister holding a familiar miniature sun.

"I saved our sun before the cleanup crews could remove it. Technically, the two systems are not compatible," Beezle said. "The helmet will overload instantly. But by that time I should have made a connection to the OverMind . . ."

"Wait!" Elara said, processing what was about to happen. "Beezle? Don't!"

Ignoring her friends, Beezle attached the two wires to the canister, channeling the full power of the miniature sun straight through the helmet and into the Arctuiaan girl.

The energy overload was enough to send a shower of

sparks from the helmet. Beezle's entire body stiffened. Her mouth opened, but nothing comprehensible came out. At the same time, currents ran through her and cascaded across Clare, who as far as anyone could tell, had no reaction to the process.

Then Beezle started spasming violently. "Unhook her!" Elara yelled.

Sabik grabbed for the helmet, but the arcs of electricity pouring off the machine struck him in the chest and sent him flying backward. Knot pushed forward, hunched over in the small room, and grabbed Beezle with both hands. The electricity poured off her stone skin without injury, allowing the Grix to reach the helmet and yank it off Beezle's head.

"Elara?" Beezle said in a voice that did not belong to her.

Elara was hesitant. Beezle no longer had the helmet on, but it was clear she wasn't herself, either. Her voice was deep and commanding, though far less harsh and rough than it had been that first night.

"Is this . . . Am I talking to the OverMind?" Elara asked.

Beezle's possessed body smiled softly. "You are talking to a voice through the OverMind, yes. It is good to see you like this, Elara. It has been many years."

"What? Who is this? Who am I talking to?"

"My time is short, and I know what you seek.

131

Answers. Answers that I can only tease."

Knot shook her head in irritation, but Elara waved to her not to interrupt.

"They were lost. Lost, and their spirits roam."

"Who? Who was lost?" Elara asked.

"Ow," Sabik added, having finally recovered from his shock.

"Someone with something to prove," Beezle whispered. The being was growing fainter. "You will taste victory. You will swallow defeat. You must read the book. You must know your enemies."

Beezle reached out and suddenly grabbed Elara's arm firmly. "Groob," she said intensely. "Find Groob before it is too late."

"Wait!" Elara called out to the entity from the OverMind. "Wait, I need to know more!"

"Who's Groob?" Sabik asked.

"I obviously don't know!" Elara snapped back. "Beezle . . . who's Groob?"

It was too late. Beezle's eyes fluttered and closed, and the small girl collapsed. Knot was ready and caught her before she hit the floor. "Beezle?" the Grix yelled. "BEEZLE? Are you okay?!"

Beezle's eyes fluttered open. She looked exhausted. Her mouth opened, and she whispered, "Clare. Need . . . Clare."

"What?" Knot said, confused. "Oh! Right. Hold on . . ."

Knot pulled the giant yellow sponge off her back and placed it on the floor. Beezle stood up weakly.

"What is it, Beezle?" Elara asked. "Does Clare have some kind of psychic power? Is that how you communicated with her before? Can she help answer the questions?"

"No . . . ," Beezle said wearily. "Shc . . . she's just . . . really soft . . ."

And with that, Beezle collapsed onto the silent and immobile yellow sponge and fell into a deep sleep.

CHAPTER 016

After all the noise from the other night, Elara was surprised they had managed to escape the building unseen. But they did, and they were back at their rooms before anyone noticed they were missing.

There was no telling how long Beezle would be asleep. Luckily, it turned out Arctuiaan mind hibernations were a cultural thing, and it wasn't too hard to get Beezle a permission slip excusing her from classes for the week. In the meantime, Elara and the rest of her friends turned their attention back to schoolwork. Or tried to, anyway. Immediately after the robot attack, things had gotten much more tense on the campus—especially after Coach Degovi had been let go. Elara didn't think the coach could really have had anything to do with the attack, so hopefully when they figured it all out, he could come back to his job.

Someone is out to get me, Elara thought to herself as she worked in the observatory on the Impossible Equation. It made no sense. How had all this happened? She just wanted to learn to terraform. And now . . . killer robots and spider monsters and . . . Elara stared at the whiteboard she had been working on. The Impossible Equation. Why was she even doing this? It was ridiculous.

The young girl sighed and crossed out a number, replacing it with a variable she had hoped might make the math make more sense. "How hard could it be," Elara asked herself, "to come up with a solution for a theorem that all of galactic civilization had decided was unsolvable?"

To Elara's complete surprise, Professor Sunderson answered, "You're wasting your time." Scowling deeper than ever, he continued: "You're treating this like it's a math problem. You'll never get anywhere that way."

Elara jumped. She had thought she was alone in the

observatory, working during a free period while her friends had a class. She had thought Sunderson was giving a lecture for another hour, or she might not have come in. She was also lucky he hadn't shown up when she was searching his desk for clues about the book.

"But . . . ," Elara stammered, caught off guard. She looked up at the whiteboard to gather her thoughts. It was covered in complex equations that she had spent all day on. "But it *is* a math problem. I mean, it's an equation . . ."

"An equation meant to represent a physical process. One with powerful ramifications. How much have you thought about this problem the headmistress has assigned you? What about practical applications?"

"I don't know!" Elara objected. "The theory of the Impossible Equation . . . it's a mass shifting and phasing of atomic values! And those values all have to be intelligently programmed . . ."

"So what would happen if you could make it work?" Sunderson prompted.

"Then an atomic cascade would sweep across a planet, transforming minerals and whatever into . . . whatever!"

"And then what?"

"Um . . ." Elara was confused. "I guess then you'd

have a terraformed planet. Except you wouldn't, because it won't ever work."

Sunderson slammed his heavy cane, hitting the ground hard. He scowled heavily. "Stop giving me excuses. The headmistress sent you here to prove yourself. She wouldn't have done that without reason. Which means you know something about this process. What is it?!"

"I don't know anything!" Elara snapped back. "The whole thing is stupid! It can't work! Even if you could somehow tell the atoms to change to other atoms, they'd just keep changing and changing! The whole thing wouldn't . . ."

Elara hesitated, looking back at the board. "I mean, it's an energy problem. So you could feed the energy from the end of the equation back into the start of the equation . . ."

"And create an infinite energy loop." Sunderson shook his head fiercely. "Put that thought right out of your mind. If you want to make things work, the conversion has to have an end. How do you stop the process once it's been started?"

Elara sagged. She just couldn't think about any of it anymore. "I don't know. I mean—"

The bell rang, for which Elara felt infinitely grateful.

Elara threw her books in her backpack. But before

she could leave, Sunderson grabbed her by the arm. "I want you to think on this, Ms. Vaughn. Make it your priority. How do you stop the process? Give me a theory, and you might just pass this class."

Elara pulled her arm free, and left.

Elara wandered down past the seashell shuttle station, along the shore of the purple ocean. In the distance she could see something massive break the surface—one of the giant creatures of Paragon. Far above, a flock of rainbow jellies fluttered through the cotton-candy clouds.

It was particularly hard to appreciate the beauty of the school. That wonderful dreamlike state Elara had arrived in had slowly been replaced by anxiety, fear, and paranoia. The stress . . . everything she had read about the glory of STS—she had never imagined the stress involved. But in all fairness, her experience hadn't really been the normal terraforming education, had it?

Elara kicked a rock. It bounced along the crystalline shore and into the calm, clear ocean. Ripples expanded where it splashed in, spreading across the surface of the water. A wave packet, the effect was called. Different waves moving at different speeds with a peak amplitude where the different waves interact. They had studied that early in the semester along with their argon gas experiments.

Is that the price of learning how everything works? Elara thought as she kicked another rock. *You don't see the beautiful ripples. No. You just see the math.* Elara kicked a third rock. Larger this time. She was angry, and kicking things made her feel a bit better. But only a bit.

The rock hit the water hard, landing with a larger splash than the previous two. The waves from the third rock were large, and swept past the first two, engulfing them.

And, just like that, Elara had it. The Impossible Equation was a wave. An energy wave, but still . . . the underlying principle . . . it was simple. So stupidly simple that Elara was sure she was wrong. So she pulled out her comm and started typing up a solution to the Impossible Equation. It didn't have to be right after all. It just had to be . . . bold.

CHAPTER 017

"**G**ood morning, friends!" Beezle announced the next day in the dorms, sitting up from the mattress she had made of Clare. Amazingly, she had no memory of the break-in to the administrator's building just a few days earlier.

"Nothing?" Elara said, feeling downcast. "You don't remember anything you said or did after you hooked yourself up to the helmet thing?"

"Not a bit!" Beezle answered cheerfully.

Elara sat down, feeling heavy. "Then it was a waste? We don't know anything else. I mean . . . except to look for the book. And that's been a dead end!" She looked up at Beezle. "I thought . . . I thought we were there to gain insight on the teachers? Get a better sense of who was responsible?"

"Ah! I see the misunderstanding," Beezle replied. "What I must explain is that the entire archive was transmitted into my head, but my head is much too small for that volume of information. And so, Clare."

"Clare what?" Elara glanced at the immobile yellow rectangle. "What about her?"

"She is a sponge!" Beezle responded happily.

"Right. I mean, I figured that out, but how does that . . . OH!" Elara smacked her forehead with her hand. "You told me before . . . She absorbs information!"

"Yes!" Beezle bounced up and down excitedly. "And her memory capacity is massive. The entirety of the archive was an easy thing to copy over into her membranes. That is why I patched her into the system with me."

"So what does she know?" Elara asked, her own excitement mounting high.

"Oh. Of this I do not know. She cannot talk, after all."

"Then . . . then how does this . . . ?" Elara sighed. "I get that you have a plan. Can we just cut to the point where you explain it completely?"

Beezle clapped her hands together. "Oh yes! I love participating in expository speeches!"

The Arctuiaan stood up and stretched. "Clare is still processing the data. I have reached her through the OverMind. Her information confirms that Sunderson has been involved in some kind of conspiracy against us, but also that he has not. It is very strange. I am hoping she can conclude more, given time."

"So, he's the bad guy though? I mean, he must be."

"I do not know. Hopefully Clare will understand more soon."

Elara strummed her fingers on the small work desk of the dorm room. "So all we can do is wait."

"Sadly, yes." The Arctuiaan tried to make a sad face, but it was almost as if she lacked the proper muscles to do anything but smile.

The conversation was abruptly interrupted by the arrival of Knot and Sabik.

"Omigosh!" declared Knot. "You're awake! I'm just so happy!" With that said, the massive Grix swept the small Arctuiaan up in her arms.

"Urk!" said Beezle happily.

"Okay," Sabik said. "So what do we know?"

Elara reiterated everything Beezle had said, which wasn't much.

"It's not super helpful," Sabik scowled. "I mean, so we suspect the guy. We already did."

"It's more than we had though," Elara replied. "It's something."

"One way or another, it all points to Sunderson," Knot said firmly. "The book that the OverMind keeps talking about was on his bookshelf. And we saw him arguing with someone."

Elara frowned, recalling her earlier encounter with the professor. "And he's been getting seriously weird about the Impossible Equation. First he was trying to push us harder, now he wants to know how we stop the equation once it's started. I don't know what he wants anymore."

"Maybe this Groob guy has something to do with it?" Sabik suggested. "Maybe they're working together?"

"Why do we not just confront him? Or talk to the headmistress?" Beezle asked.

"The headmistress thinks I'm trouble," answered Elara. "And we don't have any proof. So why would she take our word over a professor?"

Sabik sarcastically fired off a salute. "Great, so let's just go and get a book you've been trying to find for weeks. Problem solved!"

"It's not in the observatory. Chances are, it's in his private quarters. We just have to—"

"What? Break into the teachers' dorms?"

"I have a plan," Beezle said, rather unexpectedly.

Everyone turned and looked at the Arctuiaan. She looked almost serious.

"Whoever has targeted Elara is very clever," Beezle continued. "They managed to take command of the AtomiBall drones to launch an attack upon us. But, this resulted in the administration rebooting all AI on campus."

"And?" asked Elara.

"And now all the AI have been taken to the tech building for re-encryption. Acquiring a basic service bot of our own, and assuming remote control of it should be a fairly easy task."

"You're saying we can use a bot to get into Sunderson's room?" asked Sabik.

Beezle contemplated before answering. "Yes," she finally said, "I think so."

Elara clapped her hands together. "Okay. Let's—" The thought was interrupted when Elara's communicator buzzed. She glanced at the device and frowned.

"What is it?" Knot asked.

"Well, I missed Danny's call. Again." Elara

grimaced. "And I've been assigned a piloting test—a simulated trip to the moon of Paragon." Elara stood up and grabbed her backpack, slinging it over her shoulder with a deep sigh of resignation. "You guys see if you can get the robot. I'll go take care of this."

"No first-year student gets called on two field missions in the first semester of school," Knot said. "Not ever."

"Yeah, this is a trap."

"Oh! Don't go, then! Traps are bad!" Beezle warned.

Elara shook her head. "If it is a trap, that means whoever is responsible will be busy with me, right? So if it's Sunderson, you have a better chance of getting the book. Besides . . . it's just a simulation. What's the worst that can happen?"

With a half smile, she looked at the concerned faces of her friends.

"Wish me luck."

CHAPTER 018

I t was Elara's first visit to an inhospitable world—
simulated or otherwise.

The surface of Paragon's moon fluctuated between
way too cold when the sun was down and way too
hot when it was up. Gravity was about half of colony
standard, weather was unpredictable, the air was
breathable in small doses, and what little vegetation
grew on the surface was predatory and dangerous.

"Lost World," most students called it. It was the

dumping ground and petri dish for all the failed experiments of the school, many of which had added to the shifting landscape and mutated life-forms rumored to inhabit the small moon.

Elara reported to her pod—the same kind used in actual flight but with engine systems disengaged and locked down. The fact that the journey in the isolated pod was routine did not give Elara comfort. Someone was out to get her, and this was the perfect opportunity—even if the pod was programmed to stay on the planet's surface.

"Oops," Elara said in an almost convincing voice as she deliberately yanked a couple of wires from a monitor. "I seem to have accidentally uncalibrated the computer system. Looks like I'll need a different pod."

A voice spoke over the headset Elara was wearing—a seventh-year student named Thadd who was overseeing the flight. "You've only been in the pod, like, twenty seconds! How . . . ?"

Elara shrugged. "Just clumsy, I guess."

"*Pff.* Whatever," Thadd said, clearly bored with the very routine procedure. "Just pick another pod, and I'll restart the sequence."

"Any pod? Doesn't matter which?" Elara asked.

"Not to me," Thadd answered back.

"Perfect." And with that, Elara chose a lime-green-and-orange pod in the third row of the hanger. It was all she could do to ensure that her pod hadn't been sabotaged.

"Pod One, systems check is go," came the voice of Thadd through the headphones. "Activating simulated launch. Good luck, first-year. Not that you need it. This is a cakewalk."

The pod launched effortlessly into the sky, escaping the orbit of Paragon through a combination of rapid acceleration and antigravity. This, of course, was exactly the opposite of what was supposed to happen. Elara sighed. Somehow she wasn't even surprised.

"Pod One!" came the very alert voice of Thadd. "What did you do?! The mission is a simulation! Repeat—a simulation! Return control to tower now!"

Elara flicked the appropriate switches to no avail. "Tower, I have no response on control panel."

"Ah. Um . . . okay," Thadd stammered. "Okay. Just . . . I'm tracking that your pod is on course for the moon as set in the simulation. You're just . . . um . . . you're really going there. Okay?"

"No!" Elara answered, feeling the first touches of panic. "It's not okay! I don't want to go to the moon!"

"I've called in tech and Commander Bryce. So . . . okay. You're fully suited. Your pod will just return as soon as you land. If there are any problems, don't worry. You'll land near a fully stocked outpost with life support and heavy shielding. You're not in any danger. We go up there all the time. You just need to remember *kzzt!* the *kzzt!* landing *kzzt!* press *kzzt!*

Elara tapped the comm system. "Tower? I'm not hearing you . . . copy?"

Elara was met with nothing but static.

"Okay," she said to herself as she watched the view screen. "I guess my adventure begins . . . now."

The landing did go smoothly. That much was as promised. With a hiss, Elara opened the cockpit and looked out on the new planet. It was a small moon, yet Elara suddenly felt tiny. She had landed in a valley, surrounded by towering striped rocks of red and orange on top of a slightly yellow-colored mud surface.

Nowhere could she see a sign of the base that Thadd had promised. She tapped the pod's mapping system and brought up an overhead. *There it is*, she thought. *About a mile off target. Figures.*

"Tower?" Elara tapped her system. "Tower, do you read me?"

Still nothing.

Another downside: The pod's solar battery was

drained. It would take at least an hour for it to fully charge for the return trip. But, Elara noted, there was an energy signature just on the other side of the ridge she had landed on.

"Sure," Elara said to herself. "Just been hijacked off to an inhospitable moon, and someone has already been trying to kill me. Why not check out the mysterious energy blip?"

But the truth was, she was curious. After all, she was stuck on the moon for an hour. Might as well see the neighborhood, and maybe find some clues.

Elara hopped out and took an experimental step. The gravity was very different from what she was used to. She tried to hop. Not bad, she considered, covering ten feet in one bound.

A few hops later she had passed to the other side of the ridge. Elara drew her scanner. The energy signature was right on the other side of the rock. It was a weird wavelength, though, not one the scanner seemed to have in its database. Maybe an old satellite had crashed here? Or some kind of unusual radioactive mineral?

"Nope," Elara said to herself as she rounded the corner of the rock. "That's a bomb."

It was, admittedly, a tiny bomb. Maybe the size and shape of a marble, with a swirling pattern resembling smoke. It was like nothing Elara had ever seen. She would have never guessed that it was a bomb if not for the cartoonish countdown timer attached. And the bomb was set to go off in fifteen minutes.

Elara began to run. She had to get off the planet, and she had to do it now. Now, now, now.

"What's the worst that can happen?" Elara muttered. "The moon," she answered, matter-of-factly. "The moon can blow up."

Not helping myself, Elara thought. *Keep running*.

There was, of course, the small issue of the recharging battery. Elara considered a plan for that. It would involve using her suit's life support to jumpstart the ship battery. That would mean taking her helmet off for several seconds outside the ship. Still, way better than being blown up.

Elara was leaping as high and fast as she safely could, hopping across the landscape in twenty-foot arcs. All around her, the strange vegetation shivered. The plants that were growing were large and hungry.

Grabbing the stun gun, Elara blasted a vine that was reaching for her. A glance at the time took the sense of victory away. Only five minutes before everything blew up.

Another vine dropped down to block Elara's path,

and she tried to jump over it, not quite succeeding. The vine tried to grab at her tumbling body, but missed, slapping her through the air instead. *But hey*, she considered. *At least I'm rocketing in the right direction.*

Elara hit the muddy yellow ground hard and rolled. She had crested a hill and was rocketing downward super fast. She felt something tear and heard a hissing noise. Her suit. Great.

Finally at the bottom, Elara picked herself up. Two minutes. Elara was limping now, a sharp pain in her leg with every movement. A glance at her thigh and she saw the culprit—a thick thorn from the vine. She thought about yanking it out but realized she'd lose air even quicker.

Now she could see the pod. It was close, but her vision was starting to swim. She staggered. The timer ticked down, and Elara forced herself to keep moving. Each step was a shot of blinding pain.

She reached the pod. Grabbing the life-support battery that was attached to the back, she yanked it from its port. Instantly all the suit sensors went dark. Twisting the lock on her helmet, she pulled it off and dropped it. The air outside wasn't quite breathable, but the suit decompressed quickly. Better to have it off.

Elara ripped open the battery housing and pulled the two connector wires loose. Feeling a little dizzy, she pulled open the access panel to the pod battery and hot-wired the two devices together. She staggered a moment. The atmosphere was getting to her. And she was probably running out of time on that whole bomb thing, too.

She hit the hatch and practically collapsed inside. Twenty seconds left. She slammed the hatch closed and began gasping for air. Grabbing her harness and locking it in brought on a fresh wave of pain. Five seconds now. The pod was only half-charged. She hit the launch button anyway and gave a silent thank-you before she passed out as the ship jumped into the air.

Elara woke up again two seconds later as everything below her exploded into fire. The pod's systems flickered, and the ship shuddered, but she was just far enough away. The shock wave hit and pushed her further into orbit. A glance below . . .

And there was nothing. Just fire. Everything was burning.

"Pod One?" Thadd's voice rang through the comm system. "Pod One, is that you? We're getting all kinds of data. An energy signature on the surface of the moon . . ."

Elara tapped the comm switch. "Thadd. You jerk. You said this would be a cakewalk. You totally lied."

Then she passed out again and let the autopilot system guide her safely back to Paragon.

CHAPTER 019

When Elara woke up in the hospital wing, she was fully healed thanks to the school nurses. She also woke up under arrest for setting fire to the school's moon.

At her side sat Professor Sunderson.

"What . . . what?" Elara said groggily, realizing her hospital bed was behind bars.

"A necessary safety feature," Sunderson responded calmly. "Tell me, Elara. What happened on the moon?"

"I was . . . There was a bomb."

"What kind of bomb? What did you see? Did you notice a small device, then? About the size and shape of say . . . a marble?"

Elara squinted at Sunderson suspiciously. It was harder to focus than it should be. "I think I should wait and talk to the headmistress about what I saw."

Professor Sunderson looked positively sinister now. "I assure you, that would be ill-advised. It is a miracle you survived your experience. Why tempt fate further?"

Elara sat up. "Is that a threat, Professor? Are you threatening a student?"

Sunderson glanced around, taking note of the security cameras that were installed in the facility. "There are many eyes watching you, Elara Adele Vaughn," he answered softly. "Be assured that mine are amongst them."

With that cryptic statement, the professor whirled and left the room. Elara felt the tension leave her body, suddenly feeling every ache and pain from her harrowing near-death experience. She grabbed at the bars blocking her, feeling frustrated. How many times had she stayed awake at night in her home on Vega Antilles V, poring over the school's brochures and looking forward to becoming a terraformer? *Too many to count,* her mind answered. Building new worlds had been her dream . . . Not this. Not stupid conspiracies or strange mystery teachers or irritating attempts on her life. This wasn't supposed to be happening.

Elara heard the door and looked up, thinking that Sunderson might be back. Instead it was Knot, with the immobile Clare strapped to her back, followed by Sabik and Beezle.

Knot grabbed Elara in a giant hug through the bars. "Oh my goodness! I was so worried!"

"Urk," responded Elara.

"They have you in a cage? Seriously?" Sabik hissed. "My father is on the board . . . he will so hear about this."

"Are you well? Can you travel?" Beezle asked.

"I guess," Elara answered. "But I'm supposed to stay here. I don't want to get in any more trouble."

Knot responded by grabbing the bars and tearing them off. "Hush, you. You've done nothing wrong, and you absolutely cannot stay here, trapped like an animal."

"But . . ." Elara was still groggy. She was supposed to stay. And she was finally going to call Danny back. She had been a terrible sister . . .

"Listen," Sabik whispered. "Things haven't gotten

better. Another teacher's been kicked out of the school—Commander Bryce this time. The observatory was raided, too—we barely got out without being seen."

"I think they're after Professor Sunderson," Elara answered.

"What have you learned?" asked Beezle.

"He came to see me," Elara said. "Professor Sunderson. It was like he wanted to gloat? It was weird. He warned me not to say anything about the bomb—"

Knot scooped up Elara. "Talk later. We need to break into Sunderson's room and figure out what's going on."

Luckily, security was still busy searching the observatory. The plan to use a robot was abandoned in favor of speed. With the explosion on the moon and Elara breaking out of the med bay, subtlety seemed a little less necessary.

Professor Sunderson's room was cluttered. Piles of papers and clothes were stacked everywhere. And books. Most people read using a pad or comm device. It was hard to believe any teacher was in possession of so much print.

"Look at this," Sabik said, grabbing a scrap of paper

out from between a stack of books.

"What?" Knot asked. "A shopping list? We need to focus here."

"But it's a list of names," Sabik answered. "A bunch of names . . . with four crossed out. Thur'ucr. Bryce. Degovi . . . Sunderson? Why would the professor write his own name down? And then cross it out?"

"This is also curious." Beezle pointed to a closet. "Within that structure are clothes for a bipedal creature. Sunderson is not bipedal."

Suddenly, Elara spied a familiar cover out of the corner of her eye. "Found it!" With a quick movement she grabbed the book, holding it up triumphantly. *The Empire That Did Not Care.*

Elara flipped through, noticing one page was folded. With a deep whistle she pointed to an illustration. "This is *it*! The bomb on the moon! It looked exactly like this." She held up the book, showing her friends. "Now we have proof! It has to be Sunderson who built the bomb after reading this."

"Maybe," Knot said grimly as she took the book from Elara's hand and stared at the cover. "But there's something else." She glanced at Sabik.

"What?" the boy asked. "Why are you looking at me all weird like?"

Knot handed the book to Sabik, who immediately

went white. Elara took it back from him, perplexed. She opened it up and flipped idly through. "What am I looking for?" she asked uncertainly.

Knot tapped the cover. "Look closer. At the author."

Elara read the title, "*The Empire That Did Not Care*, by . . . by . . . ," and suddenly found herself at a loss for words. She looked up at Sabik, who wasn't looking back at her. Then she looked down at the book again. Then back at Sabik.

"By Sabik Suparian?" she finally whispered.

CHAPTER 020

"I never wrote a book!" Sabik yelled for what was probably the thirtieth time.

After sneaking back out of the teachers' dorms, the small group of friends had decided it was best if they all hid. There were very few options. Their own dorms were too obvious. The observatory was already off limits. And most other spaces were occupied as the staff prepared for Visitors Day. Eventually they realized the last place anyone would look for them was in the office of the headmistress herself. If nothing else, it was off the security grid.

Elara sat in the headmistress's chair, the blanket she had worn for warmth in the med bay now wrapped around her shoulders. She flipped through her comm system, off-line for the moment in case anyone tried to track the group. Behind her, Beezle tried to explain the odd but very clear reality to Sabik.

"Apparently, you did write a book. Or more specifically, you will," Beezle responded as she flipped through the pages. "The bio page is quite clear: 'Sabik Suparian, graduate of the Seven Systems School of Terraforming Sciences and Arts, author of compelling histories such as *The Lost Arts of the Xorn* and *The Trial of Gelxicon Three*, presents the true tale of the Eighth Empire—the war of the Frils and an exploration of genocide. In print for the first time!'"

"It's not me! I didn't write it!"

"But it's even signed and dated . . . ," Beezle added helpfully, holding the book open to show a picture of an aging Sabik in a tweed jacket. His hair was thin and his face was lined, but it was clearly the same person standing in front of them now. "According to this, you will write it, some fifty years in our future."

"But it's impossible!" Sabik pleaded. "Of all the

things we were supposed to find out . . . this wasn't one of them!"

"What is it that troubles you?" Beezle asked. "The theory of time travel is not alien. Though it is believed impossible, there are several equations that allow for the possibility, and even amongst the OverMind, it is understood that the essence of the hive mind extends in both directions throughout the fourth dimension."

"Not that!" Sabik exclaimed, grabbing the book and jabbing a finger at the photo. "My hairline! I'm going to go bald? Why?! It's not fair!"

Elara rolled her eyes. It was then that the plaque caught her eye. The heavy bronze one with the Impossible Equation branded into it. She moved across the room and ran her hand down the surface of the bronze plaque, taking note of the many dents and scratches. "When I first saw this . . . I thought that maybe it was old. Look how damaged it is. But the headmistress . . . she told me it was installed here when she took over the school."

Knot walked over and looked at the damage. She touched her own tongue, then tapped the bronze gently with her moist finger. "These scratches look like . . . claw marks? The headmistress must have made these scratches," she concluded.

"But why would she choose to damage this?" Beezle

asked. "Is it not a display of her achievement? The Impossible Equation changed our basic understanding of the universe."

Elara shook her head. "She failed. She failed to prove it possible. And this plaque, it's just a reminder."

"It's a bronze plaque! Who cares?" Sabik exclaimed. "How about we focus on the book? I mean . . . whatever . . . whoever wrote this, how did Sunderson get it?"

"And why would he sponsor Elara's participation in the school?" Beezle asked. "It is all quite a mystery!"

Everyone stopped and stared at Beezle. "He what?" Elara asked. "What are you talking about? I won a scholarship."

"Apparently, you did not." Beezle smiled. "I had forgotten you all lack basic telekinesis. But the data in Clare's memory systems has just been sorted. And I have discovered that Professor Sunderson personally awarded you your scholarship, long after the cutoff point. Apparently, he wanted you to be at the school."

It was a bit of a shock. So she hadn't gotten into the school on her own merits? "But why . . . ?" Elara whispered.

"Let's ask him," Knot said.

"How?" Sabik dismissed. "He's vanished. At least, according to the school's information grid. He's not in the observatory. He's not in the teacher lounge. He's not anywhere on campus."

"He's right there," answered Knot, pointing out a window toward the shuttle bay. "Looks like he's about to steal a shuttle."

Sabik quickly jumped up.

"Where are you going?" Knot yelled, grabbing Sabik by the collar of his shirt. "You can't just chase him down, we're supposed to be hiding!"

Elara shook her head. "No, Sabik's right," she said. "We can't hide forever, and if he boards a shuttle, we might never get answers!"

Sabik shook free, and soon all five friends were running down the ramp toward the hangar. Elara looked over her shoulder. Unsurprisingly, an armed security force—more than a dozen beings—were rushing toward them. *Oh well,* Elara thought. *Can't hide forever . . .*

"He's already in a ship! He's going to get away!" Sabik yelled. They had reached the shuttle bay ahead of the security forces. All five students jumped into the closest ship.

Elara threw herself down at the command seat. "No, he won't!"

"Oh no . . . ," Knot muttered as she strapped herself into a seat. "This is a bad idea . . ."

"Is something happening?" Beezle asked. "I am unaware of what our current plan entails."

"We're going to follow the professor to get some answers once and for all." Elara responded, flicking on the preflight systems. "This has to end, one way or the other."

"Then move," Sabik said roughly. "You have zero flight experience, and you haven't even stabilized the gravity systems. I've flown this kind of ship dozens of times."

Elara realized it was best not to argue. Sabik really had much more experience as a pilot. Strapping herself into the copilot seat, she watched as Sunderson's shuttle launched. Lasers blasted from the security team across the hangar. Several struck the shuttle, but by some fluke, the ship appeared unaffected.

"Hurry!" Elara urged.

"If we go too fast, he'll know we're following him," Sabik responded. "He's likely to be on the lookout for pursuit, anyway, so . . ." He tapped some numbers into the ship's comm system. "This is a backdoor circuit built into this model of ship. It allows you to patch the nav system of an identical shuttle and track its movements."

"Yeah, that's all great and stuff," Elara said sarcastically. "But there's another issue now." With that, she pointed out the side window. The security team had split off, and several of them were advancing toward the students.

"We should let them know our plans!" Beezle said enthusiastically.

At that moment, the guards began firing on the shuttle.

"What are they doing?!" Sabik yelled. "We're students! They're not allowed to shoot at students!"

"Try telling them that!" Elara yelled back.

Sabik took the hint and initiated launch. The shuttle lurched into the sky. Sparks exploded around the window from a barely deflected laser blast. The console suddenly began smoking, and electricity arced off it, sending a second shower of sparks across the shuttle interior.

"We're getting away!" cheered Beezle.

"Not for long if they keep shooting at us! Our antigravity propulsion is almost fried!" Sabik yelled back.

"I wish I had some nice calming tea," Knot added unhelpfully.

The ship rocked unsteadily through the air. Lasers strafed past the ship.

"Tea?" Elara said, twisting back to look at the Grix. "Right now? That's your one takeaway from this?"

"Tea calms me," Knot said as the ship shuddered again. "I would very much like to be calm right now."

And then the shuddering stopped. "We're out of range," Sabik said, checking the damaged instrument panel. "I can work on tracking Sunderson's signal."

Elara tapped a radar unit. "How long will that take?" she asked.

"I'd say . . ." Sabik flipped a couple of switches. "Looks like it will be done in three minutes."

"Well, that's unfortunate," Elara responded, pointing at the radar, "as the security forces are going to intercept us in two and a half minutes."

"This is so exciting!" Beezle cheered. "We are part of a real-life action film! I have always wanted to experience 'drama'!"

The ship suddenly fell into a tailspin. The surface of Paragon below began whirling.

"Why?" Elara managed to shout as she held tight to the contents of her stomach.

"It's just a temporary power loss!" Sabik shouted back. "I'll have stabilizers back . . ." The console exploded again. "Never. I will never have stabilizers back. The stabilizers are in tiny exploded pieces!"

"I want to drink so much tea right now!" Knot growled loudly through gritted teeth.

The surface of Paragon was growing closer and

closer as the ship spiraled downward. *This is it,* Elara thought. Not the ending she expected. But that stood to reason. Everything had gone bonkers the moment she left her home world. Now she was facing her fourth near-death experience in one semester. Well . . . *near* death was optimistic.

"I've got the signal!" Sabik yelled suddenly.

"How is that helpful?" Elara hissed back.

"The warp isn't off-line! I can shunt us to his location! Hold on!"

Knot glared. "What do you think we've been doing?!"

Sabik pulled a lever, and the ship suddenly stabilized, dropping into the tunnel of warp space— an established pathway set up by the Affiliated Worlds for quick travel through the depths of the galaxy.

"Okay . . . ," Sabik whispered. "Okay. We made it. Now . . . once we get to our destination, we'll be back in regular space. So we need to repair the stabilizers before we—"

But Sabik's suggestion was lost as the ship bounced back out of hyperspace, arriving at its targeted destination: Paragon's moon. As the ship once again started spinning out of control, Elara passed out.

CHAPTER 021

Several minutes later, Elara felt her eyes slowly open. The spinning had stopped, and she felt surprisingly alive.

Cautiously she wiggled her fingers. Her fingers seemed fine. Then she wiggled her toes. They were working as well. Everything still wiggled as it should. She tried to look around, but everything was blurry. "Everyone okay?" she called out.

"We are all perfectly fine," answered Beezle.

"Thanks to the heroic actions of our good friend Clare. Truly, if she had not been with us, I fear we may have all perished!"

Elara shook her head, her vision still blurry. "Wait . . . Clare?"

Elara sat up suddenly, looking around. "What happened?"

"It was amazing!" Sabik cheered. "We were crashing to the moon and Clare leapt out of the hatch! It was the bravest thing I've ever seen!"

Knot nodded. "So true. Clare dived into the ocean and used the water to transform her spongy body into its true form!"

"She was beautiful!" Beezle exclaimed. "Her giant gossamer wings unfolded, and she flew back from the ocean to the crashing ship, pulling us all to safety with her six golden arms!"

"Like some kind of super-strong space butterfly," Sabik agreed. "It was amazing."

Elara rubbed her temples and glanced at the silent, yellow, rectangular sponge. Just as immobile and lifeless as it had been since the first day of school. "But she . . . I mean . . . Clare? Really?"

Knot made a disapproving clucking noise with her tongue. "*Tsk*. Elara. You shouldn't be so judgmental."

Elara felt her cheeks burn with the comment. "You're

right, I, um . . . I'm sorry, Clare? For, uh, thinking you were just a yellow rectangle." Elara patted the yellow sponge reassuringly. "Sorry," she added again, for good measure.

Elara looked up. Her friends were staring at her, their expressions blank. Then the corners of Sabik's mouth began to twitch. Moments later, all three of Elara's best and most trusted school friends were doubled over, laughing heavily.

"Elara, come on!" Sabik laughed. "Clare is a Blossh. She's a sponge, not a space butterfly!"

Elara's cheeks burned. "Well, now you're just like . . . making fun of her. That's not cool."

Beezle smiled brightly. "Oh, Clare does not mind. The jest was her idea. We talked while waiting for you to wake up, and she was of the opinion that some light humor would help relieve tension from our current predicament."

"You mean that we crashed." Elara said, with a deep sigh, rubbing her head. She looked around. "Wait . . . the moon . . ." Elara blinked. The surface of the moon had changed dramatically since the last time she had been there. Gone was the vast, rocky jungle. In its place, a warm beach rested along the edge of a deep-looking ocean. Not far off, Elara noticed their spaceship slowly sinking into the watery depths. She was completely dry, splayed out on the beach, as were all her friends.

"How is this possible?"

"Well," a stern voice interrupted. "Look who finally showed up."

Elara and her friends all jumped. From over a sand dune a familiar round figure had emerged. "Professor Sunderson . . ." Elara scowled.

"Yes . . . and no," the professor responded with a smile. Then he pressed a small button on a wrist device he was wearing, and his form began to shimmer. Suddenly, the multi-limbed and perpetually angry-looking teacher was gone, replaced with a humanoid man in his late thirties with very serious eyebrows. The same man Elara and her friends had seen in the observatory with Professor Sunderson. "My real name is Agent Tobiias Groob, and we have precious little time. Come with me, and help save the universe."

Caught off guard by the shocking transformation, the five friends followed the agent across the sandy island. In the distance, they could see Groob's stolen shuttle craft.

"Why are we following him?" Sabik hissed to Elara. "He's our enemy!"

"Am I?" Groob responded without looking back. "Did the people who shot at me not also fire at your vessel?"

Knot shrugged. There was something to that logic. Sabik, however, looked unconvinced. "What other choice do we have?" Elara hissed at her friend. "And besides, what are we supposed to do?"

Sabik glared and pushed past his friends to trail directly behind the agent.

"Hey!" Sabik yelled, fishing the battered hardcover of *The Empire That Did Not Care* from his satchel. "Hey, Professor weirdo! Explain this!"

Without losing a step, Groob glanced at the book. "I'm an agent, actually, not a professor. That explanation I'll save for later. As for the book, it's fairly well written, though it could have used a round of editing, if you ask me. Do the galaxy a favor and enroll in a course on proper grammar before you actually write it. That will end a few troubling debates."

Sabik went pale and missed a step. Elara snatched the book out of his hand as she passed Sabik. "No . . . seriously. What's the deal with this? How can Sabik have written it? I mean . . . it would have to be from the future. And that's—"

"Entirely possible," Groob answered. "In fact, it is

one hundred percent accurate. That book, and I, are both from the future. A future that is now very much imperiled."

Elara and her friends exchanged glances. It was clear that none of them believed the agent.

"So what?" Elara pushed. "You come from the future? And you've been pretending to be a professor? It doesn't make any sense!" Elara was feeling angry now. She had been pushed and pulled and threatened and nearly blown up one too many times. "Now you act like we're just supposed to listen to you? We followed you to stop you! To prove that you're responsible for . . ." Elara gestured around at the moon. The very same moon she had been on hours before, only now it was a completely different ecosystem.

"What happened here, anyway?" Elara asked. "It all blew up! I was there. I saw the marble bomb thing explode."

"Yes, I have no doubt you did. In fact, that's what brought me here." Agent Groob reached into his pocket, pulling out a burnt-looking marble. "Is this what you saw?"

Elara took the marble. It was charred, but still . . . it had the same patterns as before. A swirl of stripes like smoke. "It . . . it looks like the same one. You found it here?"

"Not exactly," Groob said as they arrived at the ship. Next to the shuttle was a wide crater.

"Look!" Beezle said, pointing toward the center of the crater. "There are flowers growing!"

Elara stepped hesitantly toward the center. Each step revealed more and more tiny sprouts growing. Beautiful little plants that looked nothing like the monstrous flora covering the moon before. "These are . . . tribillian roses," she said with some awe in her voice. "These have been extinct for over a hundred years."

"And yet here they grow," answered Groob. "Look closer, at the center of the crater."

Elara did. There was a small orb in place. A tiny burnt sphere at the very center of the crater. A marble-size device with the same smoky pattern. Elara picked it up, gasping as she compared it to the one Groob had given her. "They're the same. The same kind of device?"

"No," Groob answered. "They are not the same kind of device. They are the same device. One exists here and now. It is the explosive you saw earlier on the moon. We stand in the exact location you discovered the bomb on your trip. But this one . . ." Groob took the first burnt marble from Elara. "This one is from the future. Just like me. Just like that book. It was given to me to prove the truth of my words."

"So what?" Sabik asked angrily. "You have two marbles that look the same, a phony book, and a really cool magic trick that turned you into . . . what, exactly? Some kind of superagent? And that's supposed to convince us you're not some kind of unhinged, murdering, moon-exploding fraud?" The Suparian turned. "I mean, no one is believing any of this, right?"

Knot looked skeptical as well. But Beezle cocked her head. "I have to admit, much of this does seem familiar."

"Familiar?" Elara asked, confused. "How can it feel familiar?"

"I think this might answer that question," Groob said, reaching into his ship. He pulled out a circular telepathy headband exactly like the one Beezle wore when she accessed the OverMind. "I will explain as much as I can," Groob continued "But truly, we have very little time. The soldiers that tried to stop our ships will not be long in tracking us. And the plan of the Frils . . . I believe Paragon is in immediate danger."

"The voices in my head . . . ," Beezle whispered, grabbing the device. "They come from this!"

"Beezle . . . ," Knot cautioned. "I don't think you should play with that thing."

"You don't understand," Beezle responded happily. "I know this machine. It is my headband! But . . . it is not at the same time. It is different."

"It is from the future as well, Miss Beezle. I understand that the proximity of it in this time zone has been causing you psychic interference."

"Yes. I think it has." Beezle turned to her friends. "Do not worry. This will explain much to us." And with that, she slipped it over her forehead. Her eyes rolled into her head, and a strange voice came from her mouth. "Hello. It is so good to see you all again," the OverMind announced. "But how little time we have, so I make my words brief." Beezle reached out a hand, and energy arced from her fingertips, cascading across Elara, and suddenly everything went black.

CHAPTER 022

Everything was dark and empty. The universe felt like one of infinite blackness. Elara felt like she was drifting alone, and yet she felt impossibly close to all of her friends. A great deal of time passed—or no time at all. It was impossible to say. And then a voice cut through. One that was Beezle and yet not Beezle.

"My friends. Let me take you to the world of Frillianth, before the time of great destruction."

Everything spun, and a planet whirled into

existence. It rotated rapidly, and Elara felt herself pulled into its orbit.

"The first species in our galactic hub to develop space travel, the Frils reached to the stars and spread across the cosmos."

The images Elara was seeing whirled around in her vision. Vast ships moving throughout the galaxy. Worlds overrun and their resources consumed, turned to fuel.

"Every world they touched became a part of their empire, a resource to be stripped and burned in the Frils' quest for dominance."

"And there was war. For the Frils were not content to consume empty worlds. They turned their appetites on all planets. Enslaving populations. Ruining cities. Destroying lives as if they were nothing. Their touch was toxic. Their breath was poison. The Frils hated all living beings. And so they set out to ensure that none stood to challenge their claim on the galaxy."

Elara could barely look. She saw buildings crumble and forests burn. Worlds that had been lush were rendered lifeless.

It was becoming harder to watch. The view whirled again. Elara felt herself drawn to the surface of Frillianth, into a stark building—a laboratory. There were several Frils at work, their wide, hulking beings wearing rubber suits that covered every inch of their bodies. Their faces were covered with gas masks and their eyes hidden behind massive goggles.

"But still the Frils plotted and planned. They would build a new weapon. One so powerful that it could destroy enemy worlds instantly, within seconds, replacing all that lived with life-forms of Frillianth design."

Elara squinted. She could see what the Frils were working on. Marbles. Tiny marbles that held an impossible achievement of science, one that would instead be used for war.

Elara felt herself pulling back into space. Before her, on the planet of Frillianth, a transformation was occurring. An explosion spread across the surface of the planet. Within seconds, the entire world erupted with an impossible amount of energy, instantly vaporizing . . . everything. The planet was gone. Without a trace.

"But the Frils did not die," the voice whispered to Elara. "The Frils were lost. Adrift in the fabric of space time. A new prison, this one of their own making. An entire world trapped for eternity between moments, able to watch but unable to interact. Until one day . . . a young terraformer made a discovery."

A new vision appeared before her eyes. In the dark,

Elara saw a being hunched over a glowing orb. It was a dizzying view, but Elara got a sense of who she was seeing. She knew who the agent of the Frils had to be.

"Sympathetic, blinded by the promise of the fabled Frillianth technology, this terraformer was corrupted beyond recognition. And soon a plan was formed that would allow the lost ones to find their way back home."

Elara shook her head. "Why are you telling me this? How am I supposed to believe you about . . . about anything at all?"

The vision faded. Elara was adrift in nothingness. She looked around, suddenly feeling at peace. The place she was in was one of calm and welcome. It felt like home.

"Hello, Elara," the voice said.

And there she was, glowing like she was made of energy, far older than Elara could have ever imagined. Her friend since the first day of school, Beezle.

"You're . . ."

"From the future," the older Beezle finished. "And I have sent my mind back in time to give you this important message. The threat of the Frils endangers us all. You must stop them from returning. Only you can do so, which is why they fear you."

"Me? Why are they afraid of me?"

Beezle smiled, the same smile she always had, now

touched with the weight of many years. "Because in the future, you are their enemy. You will lead the Affiliated Worlds into a new Golden Age, banishing the Frils from ever returning."

"But—"

The older Arctuiaan touched Elara's forehead with the tip of one ethereal finger. "There is no more time. She is about to strike, and you must not be late."

Elara felt herself slipping away, and the voice faded. "We will meet again, Elara Adele Vaughn. Many times. But for now . . ."

With a sudden jolt, Elara opened her eyes. She was back on the terraformed beach. Beezle was waking up next to her as the rest of her friends and Agent Groob hovered over them. In the distant echoes of her mind, Elara heard the final whispers of future Beezle.

". . . save the future. Save us all."

Agent Groob helped the two girls to their feet. The day had grown cold. In the sky, Paragon could be seen overhead, a bright and gleaming jewel. Elara felt the last puzzle pieces lock into place as she named her true enemy for the first time.

"Headmistress Nebulina," Elara said.

"What?" Sabik responded. "It can't be her. She's, like, one of the most respected terraformers. How could she . . ."

"It's her," Elara said. "She's an agent of the Frils. It's hard to make sense of it, but it's her. And she's going to help them by destroying a planet to give them a new home."

"But which planet? That could be anywhere!" Knot exclaimed with frustration.

"No," Beezle said with certainty. "It can only be one place. There is only one planet in the perfect location, created from scratch, placed in orbit around a lonely star."

"Paragon," Sabik whispered. "Paragon was created on a gravitational axis where all scientists agreed a perfect planet should be."

Elara's face went pale as she realized the danger. "Everyone on the planet . . . all the teachers and students and . . ."

"It's Visitors Day," Knot choked out with fear in her voice.

"Danny," Elara realized with horror. "He's probably there now. We have to stop this!"

"Then you better hurry," said Agent Groob, pointing at a streak of fire in the sky. "They've found us."

CHAPTER 023

Sabik was ripping apart the control panel of Agent Groob's ship, which much like their own had experienced damage in the escape from the hangar. Elara was watching the horizon with her binoculars. "What's taking them so long?" the young student muttered.

"Why would you even say that?" Knot glared. "It's not like we want them to find us!"

Agent Groob smiled. "I launched a decoy transponder

before landing. That'll keep them busy for a little bit."

"Professor . . ." Elara rubbed her forehead. The stress was giving her a headache. "Er, I mean agent. I still don't think I completely understand. If you're from the future, why didn't you tell me the truth from the start? I mean, we could have avoided a lot of trouble."

"Would that I could," Groob responded. "Time travel is not a simple science, and we barely understand its potential or ramifications. If I had come to you earlier, you might not have believed me. Even if you believed me, you would have no proof. And to be perfectly honest, I wasn't even sure who the traitor was myself . . . that detail was unclear in the history texts. I had to go undercover to work my way through possible suspects. It turns out you had several enemies amongst the faculty, Ms. Vaughn."

"So Thur'uer, Bryce, and Degovi?" Elara said, remembering the list they found. "Are they in on this, too?"

Groob shook his head. "Thur'uer and Bryce were suspects, but ultimately they're clean. Only Degovi and the real Sunderson, of course, are Nebulina's true accomplices." Agent Groob grinned. "Sunderson was the first traitor I detected. I learned of his treachery from Mr. Suparian's book, actually. We argued, and I decided to replace him, thinking I could find out more by working inside."

"Well, you really did a good job acting like a jerk," Elara said. "I definitely couldn't stand you."

Agent Groob smiled. "As for your so-called 'Possible Equation,' Ms.Vaughn, that was always your destiny. Not even I could stop a genius at work." Elara blushed a deep red.

"*Hrm.*" Knot grunted. "So Thur'uer's coming back then? Pity. Are you sure she's not evil?"

"She was truly unpleasant," Beezle added.

"Okay," Sabik yelled. "It's ready . . . mostly. I can't fix the impulse engines. We have to warp."

"You can't," Groob answered. "The headmistress will have blocked the warp lanes. This is her big moment, and she knows the only one that can stop it is you children. She won't risk you getting close to the planet."

Sabik shrugged. "We can get there through uncharted warp space. She can't track us there or block passage."

"But that's raw warp energy!" Knot objected. "We'll travel through The Weird! This ship doesn't have the shields for that!"

"It does now. Sort of," answered the Suparian. "I just hot-wired the reentry shields. Boosted their strength a whole bunch. Not quite regulation, but it should help."

"When did you get so optimistic about this?" Knot asked with a grim tone to her voice.

"Hey, so we're facing deadly danger? Right?" Sabik smiled. "But I'm gonna write a book. So guess what? We get to try something crazy, and we'll be okay."

"I'm not sure that's how time travel works," Beezle responded. "The underlying mechanics of paradox theory are—"

In the distance, Elara saw the intimidating shape of security forces moving across the beach toward the ship. "Party's over, everybody. They're here!" Elara interrupted. "Everyone on board! Sabik, is it ready?"

"Nope." Sabik answered as he scrambled to reattach some cable. "I need . . . maybe thirty more seconds."

"I can buy you that much," Groob said, producing a small phaser pistol from his pocket.

"What?!" Elara recoiled. "You can't do that! That gun—"

Groob pulled the trigger. A jet of water squirted out. "A harmless toy. But they won't know that. Their energy will be focused on capturing me. They won't be certain you are even here."

"Okay!" Sabik called out from the pilot's chair. "Everyone strap in! We are lifting off in ten!"

"But they'll shoot you!" Elara yelled back at Groob.

"Maybe. But I'm quick on my feet," the agent said with

a smile. "Now, go. You must stop the headmistress."

Elara tried to grab Groob as he moved away, but Knot pulled her back. "Think about Paragon! All the visitors? Your brother?"

Beezle gently pulled at Elara's hand. "Knot is correct. Groob is helping us escape. Now we must go."

Agent Groob began to run down the beach, putting himself between the security forces and the ship. Elara shook her head and climbed on board. "Okay. Let's go."

Without hesitation, Sabik started the countdown. "Five . . . four . . . three . . ."

In the distance, Elara saw the security forces pursuing Groob. His ploy had worked. But what would happen to him?

". . . two . . ."

The ship suddenly lurched forward, bouncing against a cliff wall. The engines flared, and the small transport burst through the sky.

". . . one!" called out Sabik.

CHAPTER 024

The ship blasted quickly through the upper atmosphere. Elara bit her tongue. If the trip across the planet with Commander Bryce had been scary, this was downright terrifying.

The weightless vacuum of space was unlike anything Elara had ever experienced. The regular school pods were designed for comfort. This one was meant for mid-range orbit at most. This was a rough and raw experience, and each little kick of the engine made the entire vehicle shudder.

"We have the coordinates locked in," Sabik said, looking over his shoulder at his friends. "So everyone is ready for this. You've all studied the mental effects of traveling through unshielded hyperspace. We only have a quick jump, but it might feel like a long time."

"Yeah . . . ," Elara answered, gripping the armrests of her chair. "Hold on, everyone. Things are going to get weird."

With that, Sabik activated the hyperdrive. A glowing point of light appeared before the ship. The spot brightened and widened, opening up like a tear in the blackness of space. On the other side of that rip was a kaleidoscope of whirling color—reds and blues and yellows swirling and pulsing like a living thing. It was the raw, untamed energy of the universe. So of course they were going to fly right into it.

Elara almost had a moment of doubt. Then she remembered Danny. She remembered the corner store she used to spend summer days at. The grain silo she once got locked in. The herd of wild grazizi that would sweep across the plain of her home planet every year. If the Frils were anything like they were in that vision, then everything she loved was at risk.

Sabik punched the throttle, and the ship plunged into the abyss of color. Behind them, the hole sealed shut. Elara had heard of the wilds of hyperspace—what pathfinders lovingly called "The Weird." But somehow she had always assumed it was slow and that the stories were exaggerated. Instead, the madness was sudden and everywhere.

A large group of clowns appeared in their ship.

"Okay," Sabik announced. "I know clowns just appeared. This is . . . well, it's not really normal. But it should only last a minute,"

"Clow-oons?" Beezle said, sounding out the word. "Is that what these colorful dancing creatures are called?"

"Those would be clowns. Yes, Beezle . . ." Elara shook her head, looking at a juggling green-haired clown on the windshield. That's when she noticed Knot. "You all right, Knot? You look . . . pale? I didn't think you could look pale."

The giant rock monster took a deep breath, then answered in the tiniest voice possible, "I don't. Like. CLOWNS." She shook her head. "We had these on my world. They were the darkest of beings. They hunted Grix and Kix alike."

"They're just clowns," Sabik said to bolster Knot's spirits. "It's all just makeup and tiny cars and magic tricks."

As if in defiant response, a clown hurled a giant cream pie across the cabin. Beezle saw it coming and ducked. But Elara was struck by a coconut crème. And suddenly reality melted again. The ship jumped through one vector of weirdness to another.

"Some . . . turbulence . . . ahead . . . !" Sabik yelled, his voice distorted. Elara wiped away the coconut crème and could not believe her eyes. The Suparian had suddenly become a stack of pancakes. And he wasn't the only one that had turned into breakfast. Beezle was a cinnamon bun, Knot was a stack of blueberry muffins, Clare was a waffle, and Elara had taken on the likeness of a warm lemon scone, fresh from the oven.

"I smell delicious!" Beezle said with a sniff, happy as ever.

"Don't taste yourself!" warned Elara as she ignored her sugary aroma. The blend of tart lemon and poppy seed was almost overwhelming. With great effort, she refocused on the task at hand. Crumbs of pastries rained all over.

And then suddenly everything sprang back to normal. The entire crew were seated in their chairs. There was no sign of pancakes, waffles, or the like.

"Okay," Sabik said as he wiped sweat from his brow. "We're almost through . . ."

"I should certainly hope so!" was all that Knot had to say on the subject

"I told you it would be weird!" Sabik yelled back.

"No one said I would turn into muffins!"

CHAPTER 025

With an enormous explosion of sound, the ship burst out of hyperspace exactly where Sabik had planned. They were sailing fast above the vast courtyards of Paragon where students were gathered with friends and families. It was Visitors Day, and everyone was sitting, listening to a speech by the headmistress.

"We're coming in too fast!" Knot yelled above the roar of the ship.

◀◀◀◀

Elara had to agree. The surface of the planet was growing larger at a terrifying rate. Down below, the thousands of people in the courtyard began to scream and scatter, the unmistakable sight of an out-of-control rogue spaceship enough to send everything into chaos. The ship was headed right for the podium occupied by the headmistress.

Well, Elara thought, *at least when we crash, we'll crash into the really evil person? That's kind of a win? Right?* This passed through her mind in the blink of an eye. Then suddenly the ship slowed.

"Yahoo!" Sabik shouted.

Inertial dampers built into the ship triggered the backup safety landing devices. Elara felt like her skull wanted to escape, and her stomach seemed to have fled for another star system.

The ship was floating a few dozen feet above the ground. Yes, there was black smoke billowing from the engines, and the hull was about to fall off, but everything was intact.

"Ha!" Sabik yelled. "I knew it would work!"

Elara shook her head. "How . . . ?"

"I reversed the warp field. Totally bad idea. We should have blown up across eighteen dimensions." The Suparian laughed. "Instead, well . . . we didn't!"

Beezle pointed out the cracked windshield of the

ship. "The headmistress! It is surprising that she is not running like the others."

It was true. The headmistress remained on the podium, scowling at the suspended spaceship. Elara noticed something else. Something she hoped she wouldn't see. Danny was sitting near the front row, probably wondering if his sister had stood him up again.

No time for that now, Elara thought grimly. "She's waiting for us," Elara said. "Bring us down on the stage."

Sabik didn't argue. With a pull of a lever, the entire ship shuddered and lowered itself to the platform near the headmistress. Elara pulled the hatch, and the entire door fell off. All the while, the headmistress just glared.

Stepping off the ship, Elara felt all her fears melt away. Enough was enough. She deserved some answers. Elara returned the headmistress's dark look with a single question.

"Why?"

The headmistress shook her head and smiled softly. "My dear Miss Vaughn. That is the question you have for me? Disappointing." She let out a feline-like laugh.

"I know about the Frils!" Elara said, charging forward. "And you're the puppet who wants to bring them back—"

"For the good of the galaxy!" Nebulina hissed. "You have no idea what is at stake!"

Elara felt a slight shake as Knot and her friends emerged from the ship behind her. With a rapid motion, the headmistress pulled a device from her sleeve. One press of a button, and a force field snapped into place, trapping Elara in a bubble of energy with Nebulina.

The headmistress stepped closer, pawing at the student. "Let's not allow this conversation to be interrupted."

Elara tried to step back, but the energy field prevented it. The headmistress laughed. Elara was trapped. "You really don't think you can stop me, Miss Vaughn, do you?"

"I'll certainly try," Elara shot back. "And if that was the case, why have you been trying to kill me?"

"I kept you busy. I needed you to work. To come up with ideas for my brilliant design! If I wanted you to die, I would have taken care of you myself."

"I don't understand . . ."

"Because you're a poor student," Nebulina spat. She stroked Elara's hair, gently, with her paw. Elara winced, but could not escape. "Still . . . you're the one who has made the impossible . . . possible. Can you believe it? The Frils knew. They could see from inside the time stream what would happen if I pushed you. You and your"—she licked her lips—"potential. Why else would I give such special attention to a farm girl?" The headmistress gave Elara a judgmental look. "I have to admit, I never understood why the great and powerful Frils were afraid of a child. But now having met you, I can at least understand why they would find you . . . incredibly irritating."

"I'll stop you from doing this!" Elara shouted.

"Child. This isn't about you," the headmistress said quietly. "And it isn't just about bringing back the Frils. It's about helping lives. The lives of billions who will benefit from Frillianth's amazing technology!"

"But the Frils are destroyers! What you did to the moon . . ."

"And what did you see there?" Nebulina asked. "Was the moon vaporized? Or was there life? Was there a future?"

"There was an explosion. But . . . there were plants growing . . . ," Elara conceded. "Tribillian roses."

"Extinct roses! For years I have been in communication with the beautiful Frils, and while they teach me to make weapons, I've been using their science to build powerful tools of peace! Terraforming devices that will instantly create a fully functioning bio-system!"

"But it kills everything on the planet first! Remember 'Do No Harm'? The moon—"

"That"—the headmistress waved away the concern—"was a test. One with errors. This time there will be no explosion. Nothing will die. No plants. No animals. But where I dictate, new life will grow. I've spent my whole life proving this to be impossible, but now . . . with your wave solution, it's finally achievable!"

With that, the feline removed the energy shield, stepped up to the lectern, and steadied herself at the microphone. With a slow reveal, she pulled a marble-size device from her robe and held it up to the crowd.

Elara felt her blood grow cold. She knew what she was looking at—a bomb, just like on the moon.

"Just don't!" Elara begged. "In case you're wrong. Just don't activate the device around so many beings!"

The headmistress purred, holding the small marble, and addressed the crowd with sudden frenzy. "This, my friends, this marble is the key! See how it glows. See the power within. This is a gift of the benevolent Frils!"

Elara glanced up. Her friends were horror-struck. The gathering crowd looked on with curiosity.

"Students!" Nebulina cried out, every word captured by the holo-cameras, broadcast through a gigantic and shimmering representation of the headmistress's mad face. "Witness the future! Beloved guests! See what wonders the universe has unlocked for us! For all of you will have a front-row seat to the day that everything changes!"

And with that, she pressed the globe, and it exploded with energy.

"No!" Elara shouted, shielding herself from the force.

The headmistress turned to face Elara, the dazzling light climbing in intensity.

"Don't run from this, Elara! This is the future! This is the key to a better . . . a better—"

"URK!" the headmistress said, her eyes wide with shock.

The headmistress had been right. There was no explosion this time. But the terraforming energy of the Frils had misfired. Rather than affect non-living material, it was processing the atoms of whatever it touched.

With gasps of horror, Nebulina herself was being terraformed. At a rapid pace.

Her body became water. Then stone. Then fire. As she crumbled into dust, she somehow staggered forward. Under her feet, the stage began to transform. Grass sprung up through marble. Then trees turned to water. It didn't stop there. The land continued to twist and change. The water turned to salt. The salt boiled into acid. The newly formed grass became stone and then quartz. The stage itself burned, consumed by the energy needed to fuel the atomic conversions.

And somehow the headmistress managed another step. Her hand reached out to touch Elara. The fate of Nebulina was soon to be her own.

Elara felt her knees grow weak. The headmistress—now a twisted mass of ash, reached closer and closer.

Elara's eyes closed. It was all over.

But the hand never made contact with the young girl. Instead, Elara heard a voice in her ear.

"Excuse me, Miss Vaughn," Agent Groob said. "But I believe you could use some assistance."

CHAPTER 026

Like magic, Agent Groob was suddenly on the scene, holding an unusual wand-like device covered in blinking lights and making a high-pitched whirring noise. Quickly pulling Elara aside, Groob twisted a dial on the wand and pointed it at the slowly spreading terraforming energy. Then he pointed the device straight into the air, and a thin bolt of bluish-black energy shot up into the sky.

Elara looked on in absolute wonder. She had never

expected to see a black hole with her very own eyes, hanging in the upper atmosphere of a planet. And yet, there it was. A small black hole, maybe ten or fifteen feet in diameter. More importantly, the terraformed atoms were being sucked through the hole in space.

"What are you doing?" Elara exclaimed over the roar of wind.

"Opening a portal into time space," Groob responded. "This is how I arrived in your time zone, by chrono-hopper. Now hold on . . . this part is a bit tricky . . ."

Knot, Sabik, and Beezle ran up to shield Elara. Danny followed shortly after. "Elara!" Danny cried out. "What's happening here?"

"I'll fill you in later!" Elara yelled back, her voice rising over the winds.

All the energy was being pulled from the stage, as miraculously as it had begun.

"Look how pretty it is!" Beezle said cheerfully. "I'm so happy we aren't all going to be destroyed by atomic conversion!"

"We're all glad of that, dear," Knot said, patting the Arctuiaan on the back.

"But if that's a time portal, where's all the energy going?" Sabik asked.

"Nowhere," Groob managed to respond while working. "I didn't set a destination, so the portal dumps into the time stream. Let's give the Frils a taste of their own poison."

The wand began to spark, flaring up with a yellow-and-blue energy. Groob's arm shook as he struggled to flip a switch with his thumb. The black hole was starting to grow larger now. Elara looked down and realized that her feet were off the ground.

"Uh . . . Agent Groob . . . ?"

"I know!" Groob grimaced. "The chrono-hopper was never meant to transmute this much energy!" His voice was strained, as if under a great pressure. His thumb edged forward. "Just have . . . to flip . . . switch."

And with a sudden and soft click, the beam turned white and the portal snapped shut, leaving a giant, but harmless, crater where the stage had been. After a moment of stunned silence, the entire arena erupted with cheers. Elara looked around and noticed that the audience numbered at least a thousand. The holo-projectors had broadcast every bit of action.

The agent sagged. "That took . . . a surprising amount of energy." The time wand gave off a puff of black smoke. "And it seems that it was a bit much for my poor time machine," Groob added with a look of heavy sadness.

"Wait . . . does that mean . . . ?" Elara's eyes narrowed in concern. "You can't go home?"

"Maybe." Groob shrugged. "But that's a problem for another day. For now—" He yawned. "For now I need a nap." And with that, the exhausted agent collapsed.

With the crisis over, the students and visitors of STS began to wander toward the scene. Danny looked concerned, and Elara gave her little brother a quick rundown. Nearby, her school friends reunited with their families. She saw Knot and her father, punching each other savagely in a traditional Grix greeting. Beezle leaned her forehead against the forehead of her mother, some form of psychic information being traded. Sabik was having a quiet conversation with his father, a stern-looking businessman. Even Clare had a visitor—a larger square sponge who was now sitting motionless next to her.

By the end of the conversation, Danny looked more concerned than hurt by Elara's lack of contact this semester. "So . . . are you okay? You look really hurt."

"I'm fine. I'm good," Elara said, mostly lying. "Okay, I'm mostly lying. I feel like I've been punched by an entire moon."

"In a sense that is an accurate expression of our occurrence," Beezle added, having parted ways with her mother. "Though it wasn't a moon, and it is more as if we punched it."

"Did she tell you about how we stole a ship? And flew it through uncharted hyperspace?" Sabik said, running up to the group. "It was AMAZING!"

"Wait, you did what now?" Danny asked.

Elara grabbed Danny and gave him a huge hug, ignoring the pain in her probably cracked ribs. "I'm just glad to see you. I'm so sorry I've been unavailable. I know I promised I'd be a better sister than this and . . ."

"I wasn't sure I should still come? I wasn't sure we were still close."

"Danny, no. Never." Elara shook her head. "I promise you, no matter how crazy my life gets or how long I go between holo-calls, you're still my brother." She took a deep breath. "I just . . . terraforming is crazier than I thought it would be. And . . . and . . ."

Danny smiled. "No. I'm sorry. This . . . this is you. You're doing the things you always said you wanted to do. I just get a little, y'know. Jealous. But really . . . I am just so proud of you."

With a giant rumble, Knot lumbered up behind the group, interrupting the hug. "Aw. This is all very sweet, and I do hate to break it up, but we should probably report what happened here to someone. We were just part of a planetary crisis, after all."

Elara took Danny's hand in her own. "Knot's right. I gotta go. But meet me later in the dining hall?"

Danny smiled. "Okay. Soon. I'll be waiting for you there."

Elara turned away and joined her friends. It was time to face up to whatever they had done. It was a little terrifying, facing up to who-knows-what for all that occurred, but it was still much better than—

"Hey?" Elara heard Danny call out moments later. "I think you dropped this marble? Is it yours?"

Elara spun in place. Her mouth dropped open in shock.

Danny was holding a second terraforming marble. And it was just beginning to glow. This must have been the marble Groob showed them on the moon.

Elara charged forward and tackled Danny to the ground, seizing the marble from his hands.

"What the heck?" Danny shouted. "I'm just trying to help."

"No time for that now," Elara shot back. "We're in trouble!"

The second marble was warm, and getting warmer. The atomic conversion process had clearly begun. But Groob was passed out, and his time wand was melted. And most of the crowd had dispersed for the day.

"The force field!" Elara shouted.

Sabik was stunned. "We . . . we can't. It was wrecked when the headmistress was destroyed!"

"A containment device, then!" Knot yelled back. "Like the miniature sun!"

"There's no time," Beezle said. "And the energy output is too high."

"I don't understand!" shouted Danny. "What's wrong?!"

"A second terraforming device! And it's about to blow! We have to do something!"

Beezle considered. "According to Sabik's book—"

"I didn't write that book!" Sabik yelled back.

"The chemical reaction can be neutralized with acid. Oh! Like our experiments. How very interesting!"

"But we don't have any acid!" Sabik yelled back. "We have to get it off the planet! And we have to do it now!"

"How?" Knot responded. "The ships are destroyed."

Elara looked at Danny. "Run," she said. "Run as far as you can, and hold on for dear life!"

There wasn't long now. The plastic was boiling away. Soon she would suffer the same fate as Nebulina. Elara wondered what it would feel like to have her atoms transformed. It was just too much. To lose her planet and her friends . . .

If only there was something that could stop the chain reaction. Some kind of containment system. Some kind of acid . . .

Elara looked down. The marble was about to explode. So the first-year student did the only thing she could think of. It might not save the world, but it was better than nothing.

Elara Adele Vaughn swallowed the marble.

CHAPTER 027

Several minutes passed, and Elara did not explode. This was of great relief to her.

Eventually the local authorities arrived, along with a medical team and the rest of the faculty. The newly rehired Commander Bryce and Professor Thur'uer were in tow, and all were worried sick over the fate of the girl. Elara was mystified, and a little bit scared, but by some sort of miracle her scans came back clean. There were slight signs of elevated cellular activity, but otherwise the marble was neutralized by her stomach acids.

Paragon and the Seven Systems School of Terraforming were safe, thanks to quick thinking and digestive juices.

Commander Bryce and Professor Thur'uer ran forward. "I told everyone what happened," Thur'uer said. "We saw it all!"

"Yes," admitted a somber Commander Bryce. "So very tragic. That Nebulina would resort to such measures because of her pride. I am so very sorry that you children were caught up in this tragedy."

"And so very glad you survived!" added Professor Thur'uer. "This is when we see the dangers of such careless experimentation! Why, if we don't stop such—"

Commander Bryce held a hand up and silenced the reptilian teacher. "Yes, not now, Professor Thur'uer. The point is, you have all come back safely and in one piece."

"But we're still expelled, right?" Elara said glumly.

"What? No! Of course not!" The professor looked aghast at the very idea. "You five have proven to be some of the brightest and bravest students this school has ever been honored to have in attendance! And you saved a world! That matters, young miss!"

"Well done, comrade." Commander Bryce saluted.

"Now, why don't you all go and get some rest. There will be many questions for a later time," Thur'uer continued. "Emissaries from the Galactic Council will be speaking to you all in the morning. But for now, we will celebrate your safe return. Go to your dorms. Rest a bit. I'll send a message when it's time for the feast."

The crowd parted, and Elara and her friends made their way through the throng of excited students who clapped and cheered. Of all things that Elara expected when she returned to STS, this was not on her list of possibilities.

She had left her homeworld, but she had found her home.

For the first time in what felt like an eternity, she felt her heart stop pounding in her chest. The Impossible Equation. The vague threats. The isolation.

Finally, she could just be a regular student. Finally, she could learn her arts and make the galaxy a better place.

"It's over," she whispered to herself.

EPILOGUE

Meanwhile, in the depths of the time stream . . .

The Frillianth council watched all that had transpired. The fall of the headmistress, the meddling of the time agent called Groob. Elara Adele Vaughn's victory. The defeat of their technology.

The Frils showed no emotion—they couldn't in their weakened state. But every one of them felt the same burning anger. It had taken Fril scientists thousands of years to find a weakness within their temporal prison. Reaching backward through time and rewriting history had taken a staggering amount of work. All for nothing.

There was one thing for sure. Elara would fall. She would not lead the war against the Frils in the future. One agent had fallen. One plan had been foiled. But the Frils were patient and the Frils were wise. A thousand more plans stood ready to launch.

Soon there would be a new galactic order.

KEITH ZOO is an illustrator living in Boston, Massachusetts. For the past decade, he's been the Lead Artist at FableVision Studios, working on a full range of things from character design and animation layout, to interactives and design. When he's not doodling monsters, goblins, and other silly things, he's spending time with his wife and baby girl. To check out more of Keith's work, head on over to keithzoo.com.

LANDRY Q. WALKER is a *New York Times* best-selling author of comics and books. His work includes Star Wars stories, Batman and Supergirl comics, and the book you are holding in your hands. He likes castles and robots and also Pop-Tarts. Most days he hangs out with his cats and pushes buttons on a keyboard until stories somehow happen.

The adventures continue in

Coming in 2018.